Reprint Publishing

FOR PEOPLE WHO GO FOR ORIGINALS.

www.reprintpublishing.com

New
Waggings
Of
Old Tales

BY

TWO WAGS

ILLUSTRATED BY OLIVER HERFORD

BOSTON

TICKNOR AND COMPANY

211 Tremont Street

1888

𝔘𝔫𝔦𝔳𝔢𝔯𝔰𝔦𝔱𝔶 𝔓𝔯𝔢𝔰𝔰:
JOHN WILSON AND SON, CAMBRIDGE.

Dedicated

TO

FRANK DEMPSTER SHERMAN,	JOHN KENDRICK BANGS,
BY HIS TRULY,	*BY HIS FRIEND,*
J. K. BANGS,	F. D. SHERMAN,
who seizes this opportunity to inform his friends that he is in no way responsible for the verses which have crept into the following pages.	*who begs to acquaint the public with the fact that the prose portions of this work have been inserted against his expressed wishes and in defiance of his advice.*

LIST OF ILLUSTRATIONS.

PROLOGUE.

T seemed a fairly good idea.

The children were to be given an entertainment, and some one suggested that an authors' reading of the tales of childhood be tried, provided the authors were willing. Unfortunately investigation showed that the authors were all dead, otherwise they would doubtless have assisted gladly.

It was then proposed that such kind gentlemen as the Eminent Realist, the Distinguished Diplomat, the Illustrious Laureate, and others should be asked to read the stories for the dead authors, and happily they were unanimously willing.

So it happened. The children gathered, and in their hands were placed daintily-printed programmes setting forth in all the glory of æsthetic type that "'Hop O' My Thumb' would be read to them by the Eminent Realist; that the Apostle of Obscurity would recite a myth; that the Leader of the Fleshly School would charm their ears with the 'History of Mary and the Lamb;' that the Disciple of Ambiguity would tell of 'Jack and the Beanstalk;' that the African Reminiscencer would recount the thrilling story of Rumpelslopogaas; while 'Beauty and the Beast' and 'Cinderella' would be treated respectively by the Great Romancer and the Illustrious Laureate." By common consent the chairman of the occasion was to be the Distinguished Diplomat, whom the children universally admired because of his familiarity with his mother tongue and every one of its ancestors, dead or otherwise.

The day was propitious; none of the proxy authors disappointed, and the proceedings were exactly as they are set down in the following pages.

E must be a strong combination of un-interesting vacuity and fatuous imbe-cility, or must have been sent into the world unfurnished with that modulat-ing and restraining balance-wheel which we call a sense of the beautiful, who in his old age is unable to appreciate with all the ardor of youthful enthusiasm those ever-inspiring yet simple tales which have been handed down, almost I might say *ab urbe condita*, to us, our children, *et nati*

natorum et qui nascentur ab illis, without being accused of going *extra muros
veritatis*.

" *Vive le roi!* was an expression com-
monly used in France in the days prior to
the great Revolution, — *ante bellum* days,
as the Latins so beautifully termed them.
May I not adapt to the present occasion
this undying line from French literature,
and cry from the depths of my heart, *Vive
le Fairoi?* I think I may.

"As I have frequently remarked on
other occasions, I should have preferred
that this office I am to perform to-day
had fallen to another. It has been many
years since I have

> ' Dag an' delf in
> Impe and Elfin,'

as our great — I should say England's
great — poet Chaucer might have said
upon a similar occasion, had he been

called upon to stand *in loco moderatoris* to so enlightened an assemblage as I see before me. There are others who are better fitted than I to act in this capacity ; but as I have made it one of the invariable rules of my life *nec quære nec spernere honorem, — ich dien.*

" Not to detain you longer than is necessary, — for, as Bacon has said, when things are come to the execution there is no secrecy comparable to celerity, — I will introduce to you the Eminent Realist, with whom, in accordance with the scriptural prophecy, 'By their works ye shall know them,' many of you are doubtless already familiar. The distinguished gentleman has kindly consented to lay before us the particulars of the pathetic career of 'Hop O' My Thumb.' "

After the applause which greeted these remarks had subsided, the Eminent Realist, adjusting his necktie and taking his manuscript from the upper right-hand pocket of his coat, advanced to the edge of the platform and read: —

THE RISE OF HOP O' MY THUMB.

WHEN Barclay Williams went to interview Hop O' My Thumb for the "Solid Men of Fairy-land" series which he undertook to finish up for the "Decade" after he had paid the debts of that newspaper and acquired its ownership, My Thumb received him in his private office by previous appointment.

Barclay hesitated, as he entered the door, whether he should wipe his feet on the mat or not. To be sure there was a sign requesting him to do so pinned upon the upper left-hand panel of the door, but a large sea-green inscription, WELCOME, upon the mat itself seemed to forbid any such familiarity. Unfortunately his embarrassment was considerably augmented by Hop O' My Thumb himself, who, upon hearing a footstep without, cleared his throat and pushing his chair backward about two feet from his desk began to wonder whose footstep it was. He thought he recognized the squeak of the shoes as belonging to Barclay, but he was not certain enough on the point to come to any definite conclusion; so turning half way round he arose from his chair and started to walk toward the door, glancing furtively at the transom as he did so.

" Come in," he said.

Barclay still hesitated.   There was something in Hop O' My Thumb's tone that con-
tributed further to his uncertainty on the
question of the door-mat.   If he wiped his
feet on My Thumb's WELCOME, My Thumb
might be angry; on the other hand, if he
disregarded the warning on the door-panel
he still might give offence.   A hurried
glance at his shoes decided him.   They were
not at all muddy, and then he remembered
that he had come from his house in a cab
and that the shoes were new.   He smiled
quietly to himself, and remembering his
early athletic successes at college he jumped
easily over the mat and found himself
confronted by his host, whose misgivings
as to whether or not Barclay was a creditor
had led him to put on his seven-league
boots in the interval between his invitation
to enter and the entrance of his guest.

" Oh, it 's you, is it? " said Hop O' some-what absently, spurning a three-legged stool across the room to where Barclay stood and motioning to him to be seated.

" How did you guess? " asked Barclay, surprised at this sudden recognition.

" I don't know," replied Hop O' My Thumb with charming *naïveté*. " Because you look so like yourself, perhaps, or be-cause you —" then he stopped and fondled his watch-chain nervously. It was evident that he could not think of any other rea-son. Barclay felt his embarrassment com-ing over him again, and inadvertently broke the end of his lead-pencil.

" What do you want, young man? " con-tinued My Thumb, recovering his com-posure with some apparent effort.

" Your life," said Barclay. " We want the lives of all the great men of Fairy-land for the 'Decade.' "

Hop O' My Thumb was somewhat startled at Barclay's first words, and a nervous movement of the legs placed him some distance from the Interviewer. He had forgotten to remove the seven-league boots. Another nervous twitch, however, brought him back to Barclay's side in time to hear his last words. Barclay wondered at this sudden disappearance and equally sudden reappearance of his host, but he was too well bred to express any surprise. He merely made a mental note of it for the treatise on the Eccentricities of Genius, which he was preparing for a future number of the " Pacific Monthly."

"We want to hear about this Ogre business, you know — and — " here Barclay faltered ever so slightly. He was a Bostonian, and he was proud of it, but he did not want to appear too proud. With much effort he finished his sentence, however. "And how you were befriended by the — the beans." Barclay blushed.

Hop O' My Thumb looked at him silently and then laughed. He was amused at the Interviewer's embarrassment, and made no effort to conceal it.

"All right," he said; "where do you want me to begin?"

"Might begin with your poor but honest parents," suggested Barclay, elevating his eyebrows.

A smile betrayed that Hop O' My Thumb possessed a sense of humor. He had read the life of his neighbor John the Slayer of Ogres, in the preceding number of the "Decade," and he appreciated Barclay's satirical allusion to the opening chapters of his rival's life.

"Well," he replied sadly, "I had 'em."

"Seventeen children, all girls except the boys, I suppose," Barclay cut in.

"Yes, seventeen, and all girls except the boys," repeated Hop O' My Thumb, accepting Barclay's flippant query as fact. It was not fact, but then Hop O' thought that if Barclay was satisfied he ought to be; and then, too, Barclay knew just what the readers of the "Decade" wanted, while he did not.

"Hop O' My Thumb," wrote Barclay, "was the son of poor but honest parents. There were seventeen children in the family, all of whom were girls except — by the way, how many brothers had you?" he asked, laying down his pen.

"Seventeen, I think you said," replied Hop O' My Thumb, throwing his left leg across his right knee.

"Oh, come now!" ejaculated Barclay, a little out of patience. He did not like to be balked so early in the interview, and he could not help feeling that perhaps

Hop O' My Thumb was making game of him. "You just said they were all girls except the boys."

"Well," replied Hop O' My Thumb, "so they were. But we were all exceptions in my family. It was an exceptional family, you know."

"Very well," returned Barclay, with a comical look of resignation in his face. "Go on and tell me all about it. You were the biggest of the lot, I presume," he added sarcastically.

"I think, Mr. Williams," replied Hop O' with a quiet dignity, "that if you intend to make this a satirical article you would do better to leave me out of it."

"Oh no," said the Interviewer, un-abashed; "a biography of Hop O' My Thumb with you left out would be like Boston deprived of the east wind."

"Hop O' My Thumb," wrote Barclay, "was so diminutive in stature that his progenitors conferred upon him the ap-pellation by which he is now so generally and popularly known. But Nature, as if regretting the exigencies which had compelled her to make him physically weak, had more than compensated him by the psychical strength with which she endowed him.

"There," he added, putting his pen behind his ear, "how does that go?"

"Very well indeed," was Hop O's enthusiastic rejoinder. "It is the most expressive and eloquent way of saying, 'Little, but oh my!' I have ever seen. Are you going to write the whole of this life in words of ten syllables?"

"One must be original," said Barclay, apologetically; "and besides, it must be made so that children will comprehend and be instructed by it."

"Of course," said Hop O'. "I've noticed that all the one-syllabled editions of my reminiscences have had to be elucidated by very highly-colored cuts. Yours is not an illustrated paper, I believe?"

"No, I'm happy to say it is not," replied Barclay a little impatiently.

"I'm sorry about that," said My Thumb, reflectively. "It would have seemed more homelike to appear in an illustrated weekly. Father was a wood-cutter, you know."

As Hop O' My Thumb spoke these words the door-bell rang and he excused himself for a moment to answer it. In the interim Barclay numbered the pages of his manuscript consecutively, and leaning back in his chair jotted down a few lead-pencil notes.

"Children retire to bed."
"Hop 'O My Thumb suffers from insomnia."

Barclay chuckled as he wrote this.

"Too short to sleep long, I suppose," he remarked to himself. Then he wrote, —

"Overhears parents weeping because of shortness of the larder."

" Hop decides to prepare for the worst, and pockets the next day's bean supply."

When Barclay had written thus far the point of his pencil broke, and while he was meditating whether or not to re-sharpen it, Hop O' My Thumb returned. Barclay watched him curiously as he en-tered, and noticed that his host took par-ticular pains to elude the door-mat, just as he had done. He was secretly pleased that he did so. It made him feel more at his ease than he had felt at any time since he had entered the house.

" Back again? " he asked quietly, as Hop O' My Thumb entered.

" I don't know," retorted Hop O' My Thumb, absently. " What? Oh yes. I beg your pardon, I was thinking of some-thing else. Yes, I'm back again. How far have you got ? "

" I have reached the point where you

surreptitiously removed the beans from the larder," replied Barclay, glancing at his notes.

" They were n't beans, Mr. Williams, they were pebbles," said Hop O' My Thumb, gazing at Barclay with astonishment.

" Oh, I know that. But we 've got to give it a touch or two of local color — a contemporaneousness, you know."

" Well, it seems to me that it 's a contemporaneousness that I don't know, and don't care to know, that you 've got hold of. If you think I 'm going to cut off entirely from my past you 're mistaken, and if you don't want my life as I lived it you must n't come to me for points. Go to the newspapers."

" Well, well, have your own way. Pebbles it is — pebbles it are — pebb— "

" Never mind," said Hop O' My Thumb, kindly, " if pebbles mix you up so, make it beans. I took the beans, and when my poor but honest parents lost my nineteen brothers and myself in the woods, I dropped the beans one by one along the roadway, and when night came on, with the aid of the street lamps and the beans together, I led my ten sorrowing little relatives back to their home, much to the surprise of my father and mother, who were having an oyster supper in honor of their bereavement as we entered."

Barclay stroked his chin and blushed. Why he did the former he knew not, but for the latter he could readily account. He felt that some one should blush for such inconsistency and patent perversion of fact as he had just listened to, and as Hop O' My Thumb showed no disposition to do it, he thought it his bounden duty to assume his host's responsibilities.

"Mr. Hop O' My Thumb," he said gravely, after some moments' reflection, "do you wish street lamps introduced into this biography?"

"Why not? Are n't they contemporaneous enough?" queried Hop O', biting off the end of his cigar and drawing a match slowly across the sole of his shoe.

Barclay gazed out of the window. He perceived that in spite of the fact that he had been graduated at Harvard, in spite of the fact that he lived on Beacon Street and knew who his grandfather was, Hop O' My Thumb had him. It galled him considerably, but he was too sensible a man to let My Thumb see the true state of his feelings.

"All right. Please continue," was all he said.

Hop O' My Thumb resumed: —

"Mother was glad to see us, and father

with some embarrassment asked us when we got back. I made some inopportune reply, to the effect that we had returned the very moment we arrrived, which so enraged father that he sent us all to bed without any supper. The next day we were conducted to the forest again, but not before I had taken the precaution to empty my little missionary bank of its contents, which, for the want of pebb— I beg pardon — beans, I dropped along the road. Unfortunately I failed to notice that father walked behind me, picking up the dimes and nickels as I dropped them."

At this point Hop O' My Thumb was visibly affected, and Barclay not wishing to intrude upon his grief, went across the street to purchase a cigar.

When he returned, Hop O' had regained his wonted composure, and offered Barclay a light. This the newspaper man graciously accepted, and placing his hat upon the mantel-piece he reseated himself at the desk.

"That night," said Hop O' My Thumb, "all thirteen of us were irrevocably lost."

"Thirteen is an unlucky number," suggested Barclay, with a vain hope of driving Hop O' back to the original number of brothers.

"I know it; but don't you think it makes the story more weird and interesting?" replied Hop O'. "You might also say that the missionaries lost thirteen dollars by my foolishness and my father's watchfulness, if you think it would add to the story. Of course," he resumed, "it rained that night, and as luck would have it all the boys had brought their canes. There was not a solitary umbrella in the whole party. That adds another item to the long list of mishaps attendant on thirteen.

It is very unlucky for thirteen men to be out in a rain-storm with canes."

" It is," said Barclay, looking despairingly at Hop O'. " Suppose we let the number drop? It may kill one of us."

" As you please," responded My Thumb, good-naturedly; "half that number of brothers is enough for me."

" What did you do when the rain came on?" asked Barclay, not unmusically knocking his pencil against his teeth.

" Let her come," flippantly replied My Thumb with a pleasant smile, which displayed a fine white set of teeth of which their owner was justly proud.

" I knew that," was Barclay's indignant response, " but what else did you do?"

" Got wet," replied My Thumb, his smile extending into a loud guffaw. Then noticing a look of pained surprise on his caller's face, he hastened to add, " We pulled the bell-knob of a solitary castle that we perceived on the neighboring moor. The bell responded, as I rather suspected it would, and after a temporary lull of say five or ten minutes, the lady of the house appeared and earnestly requested us to move on."

"And you moved?" queried Barclay, pulling at his trousers to keep them from bagging at the knees.

"Not an inch," said My Thumb with dignity. "We moved in, the whole six and a half of us —"

"Now, see here," interrupted Barclay, his ire again rising; "what do you mean by 'six and a half of us?'"

"I thought we settled on it that thirteen brothers were at least twice too many?" said Hop O'.

"Well, we did, but six and a half is such an odd number," rejoined Barclay, irritably.

"Not at all," said Hop O'. "If it were seven or five it would be an odd — "

"Oh, I don't mean that way," retorted Barclay, tapping the oil-cloth with his toe. "You could n't have six and a half brothers; the idea is absurd."

"I don't see why," replied Hop O', with an injured look. "A man can have a half-brother, I believe, can't he?"

Barclay was silent. Hop O' My Thumb's statement admitted of no denial, so he thought it best to appear satisfied at the turn things had taken. After an interval of some minutes Hop O' My Thumb resumed: —

"We were rather sorry after we had entered the house so unceremoniously, as we found it belonged to a gentleman whose chief delight consisted in the devouring of little boys on the half-shell. Mrs. Ogre gave us a chance to leave the place before

her husband returned from the Museum,
where he displayed his physical peculiarities to the populace at a dime per head;
but before we could get out of the house,"
— Hop O' My Thumb called it *heouse*, —
' the proprietor walked in hungrier than a
girl of sixteen after a german."

"Is she anything like an American girl
of thirty after an Englishman?" queried
Barclay, flippantly.

"Fortunately," continued Hop O', with
a scornful smile at the Interviewer's sally,
"the ice-chest was large, and we managed
to hide before the Ogre came into the
room. But our fancied security did n't
last long.

"'Do I smell any little boys around
here, madame?' the Ogre asked of his
wife.

"'Yes, husband,' said the poor woman,
'there is a little cold youth downstairs,

left over from Sunday's dinner. I — I — I thought you'd like it hashed for tomorrow's breakfast,' she added.

"'All right,' replied the giant; 'I'm glad you have it, for little boys are out of season just now, and I can't get any nice ones in the market. Hello! what's that?' he added sharply.

"It was a very unfortunate thing, but my youngest brother, boy-like, had constructed a slide on one of the Ogre's ice-cakes, and while indulging in youthful sport he fell, making such a noise that our presence was revealed. We were very much frightened, and offered to let the Ogre have our little half-brother if he would let the rest of us go; but he was adamant."

"That's hard," cut in Barclay.

Hop O' My Thumb got up from his chair, and crossing the room opened a

drawer in the small mahogany escritoire
which stood opposite the window. After
rummaging around among his papers
for a few minutes he picked up a small
pocket edition of Webster's Dictionary,
and turned rapidly over the " A " pages
until he came apparently to the word
he wanted. He then replaced the book
where he found it, and locking the drawer
returned to his chair. Barclay gazed at
him wonderingly for a moment and then
asked, —

"Well?"

"You are right," said Hop O', "adamant is hard."

Barclay smiled wanly. It was all he
could do, and he did it as wanly as he
knew how. He saw that Hop O' My
Thumb had missed his true vocation in
life and it saddened him. He tore a small
bit of paper from the edge of a sample

copy of the "Decade" that he always carried with him, and threw it pensively into the waste-basket.

Hop O' for the first time during the interview seemed embarrassed. The thought flashed across his mind that he had gone too far, and he was repentant. It was some moments before he spoke again, but when he did speak there was an indescribable tenderness in his voice that Barclay had not given him credit for.

"Then," he said softly, "we were filed away upstairs to fatten, and to those who know us it is needless to say that we did fatten."

"It is not a laborious task to fatten at another's expense," said Barclay in parenthesis.

"The night before the festival at which my brothers and I were to be served,"

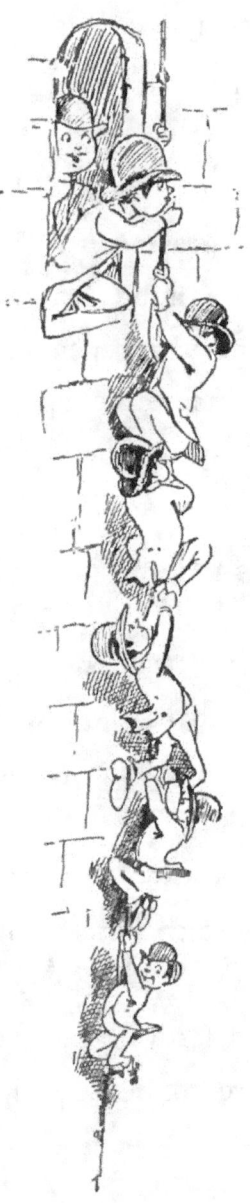

continued Hop O',
resolved to ignore
the insinuating re-
marks of his visitor,
" I bethought me
of a method of es-
cape. I hurriedly
dressed my family
up in the clothing
of the Ogre's daugh-
ters, and when the
butcher came that
night he immolated
the young ladies in-
stead of us, and we
climbed down the
lightning-rod into the
moat and took to
the woods. The next
morning, when the
Ogre discovered the
trick we had played

on him, he was very much annoyed, so he put on his seven-league boots and started after us. But I had a *ruse* for him."

"A Charlotte russe, I suppose," put in Barclay, dryly.

"No," rejoined Hop O', "not a Charlotte russe; we could n't sponge cake enough for that. We six and a half brothers each took a different route, and the Ogre got so tired trying to make up his mind as to which of us was the most luscious that he fell asleep. Then came my chance. I was on friendly terms with the sea-serpent at the Ogre's Museum, and I knew he was jealous of the Giant whose name was printed in larger letters on the bills than his. I immediately despatched my half-brother to him with word to come to me at once with his stinger. He came, and was only too glad to fasten his fangs on the Ogre, who died in great agony about two hours later."

"There is no poison like jealousy," said Barclay, whistling a low tune to himself.

"No, indeed; and the sea-serpent is a good deal of a green-eyed monster, you know," replied Hop O', relighting his cigar. "I searched the Ogre's pockets and found a certified check for all his wealth, payable to bearer, with a signed deed to all his property in blank. I felt rather sorry for his wife. She had been very good to me during my sojourn in her husband's castle, and I was instrumental in her losing her children; so after I had had the transfer recorded, and had cashed the check, I got her appointed to a postmastership in Oregon, where she gets a commission on the stamps she sells."

"Of course you sought out your father and mother after acquiring all this wealth?"

said Barclay with a sigh of relief that the biography was so nearly completed.

"Well, ahem!" replied Hop O', nervously, "the fact is I — ah — by the way, take a handful of these souvenir pebbles," he said, turning away his head to hide the blush which suffused his cheek, and taking half a dozen small stones from his pocket.

"Hop O' My Thumb has been known to blush," wrote Barclay in his note-book. Then he said "Pebbles? What are they for?"

"Oh, they helped me find my way home. They may help you to find yours," returned My Thumb, pointing toward the door in a suggestive manner. "You ought to write up this interview while it's fresh, and you doubtless wish to get to work on it."

Hop O' My Thumb said *woyk* for work, but Barclay understood him nevertheless.

"Yes," he said, "I do wish to get to work on it, although an interview as fresh as this has been will keep a long time;" and then he slammed the door violently and was gone.

"If that man makes me out a Munchausen, I'll kill him!" said Hop O' My Thumb, getting up and throwing his cigar-stump out of the window.

GAIN the Distinguished
Diplomat stepped to
the edge of the plat-
form and wished
that some one
else had been
called upon to
perform the pleasant duty of introducing
the readers. "For," said he, "I have
never been afflicted with the *cacoëthes
loquendi*, — indeed, what *cacoëthes* I have
is more *scribendi* than otherwise. But *bon
gré mal gré je suis ici tout de même.*

"The great Leader of the Fleshly School
whose name is next *sur le tapis* was in-

vited to wag for us *à discrétion* the tale of
Mary's Lamb; but a glance at the manuscript a·few moments since convinced me
that the *beaux esprits* of the poet had led
him to adorn the tale with a few face-
tious flights of fancy unfitted to the present occasion.   However, *humanum est
errare et, mutatis mutandis, revenons à
nos moutons.*"

The Poet, blushing deeply, bowed to the
audience and began.

MARY AND THE
LAMB.

MARY, — what melo-
dies mingle
To murmur her
musical name !
It makes all one's
finger-tips tingle
Like fagots, the food of the flame :

About her an ancient tradition
   A romance delightfully deep
Has woven in juxtaposition
   With one little sheep, —

One dear little lamb that would follow
   Her footsteps, unwearily fain,
Down dale, over hill, over hollow,
   To school and to hamlet again ;
A gentle companion whose beauty
   Consisted in snow-driven fleece,
And whose most imperative duty
   Was keeping the peace.

His eyes were as beads made of glassware,
   His lips were coquettishly curled,
His capers made many a lass swear
   His caper-sauce baffled the world ;
His tail had a wag when it relished
   A sip of the milk in the pail, —
And this fact has largely embellished
   The wag of this tale.

One calm summer day when the sun was
   A great golden globe in the sky,
One mild summer morn when the fun was
   Unspeakably clear in his eye,
He tagged after exquisite Mary,
   And over the threshold of school
He tripped in a temper contrary,
   And splintered the rule.

A great consternation was kindled
   Among all the scholars, and some
Confessed their affection had dwindled
   For lamby, and looked rather glum :
But Mary's schoolmistress quick beckoned
   The children away from the jam,
And said, *sotto voce*, she reckoned
   That Mame loved the lamb.

Then all up the spine of the rafter
   There ran a most risible shock,
And sorrow was sweetened with laughter
   At this little lamb of the flock ;

And out spoke the schoolmistress Yankee,
　With rather a New Hampshire whine,
" Dear pupils, sing Moody and Sankey,
　Hymn ' Ninety and Nine.' "

Now after this music had finished,
　And silence again was restored,
The ardor of lamby diminished,
　His quips for a moment were floored.

Then cried he, " Bah-ed children, you blundered
  When singing that psalmistry, quite :
I 'm labelled by Mary ' Old Hundred,'
  And I 'm labelled right."

Then vanished the lambkin in glory,
  A halo of books round his head :
What furthermore happened the story,
  Alackaday ! cannot be said.
And Mary, the musical maid, is
  To-day but a shadow in time ;
Her epitaph, too, I 'm afraid is
  Writ only in rhyme.

She 's sung by the cook at her ladle
  That stirs up the capering sauce ;
She 's sung by the nurse at the cradle
  When Ba-ba is restless and cross :
And lamby, whose virtues were legion,
  Dwells ever in songs that we sing,
He makes a nice dish in this region
  To eat in the spring !

———

"ONG experience in public life," said the Distinguished Diplomat, "has taught me that ambiguity is the mother of success. The Venus of Milo is doubtless more satisfactory to a large majority of mankind with her arms buried in oblivion than had she been found with those desirable adjuncts at her side. There is a pleasing uncertainty about them. Were they graceful, or were they not ; were they plump, or were they lean? In fact the old, old question arises — was it the Lady or the Tiger?

" The poet spoke truly who said, *Medium tenuere beati*. Indeed, happy is this Disciple of Ambiguity, who has kept the middle course, and has permitted his readers to adopt his means to justify their ends. Will the ambiguous gentleman kindly begin? "

There was nothing equivocal in the Disciple's acquiescence, for he at once began to read.

THE DISCOURAGER OF CURIOSITY.

IT was nearly a year and seven weeks after the occurrence of that event in the arena of the semi-barbaric Potentate known as the incident of the Beauty and the Beast, that there came to the Bungalow of this Tyrant an Investigating Committee of five commissioners from the State of Michigan. These men, of venerable and dignified as-

pect and demeanor, were received by the
Second Deputy Vice-Vizier of the Dead
Letter Department, and to him they made
known their errand.

"Most noble Office-Holder," said the
speaker of the deputation, "it so happened that one of our
fellow-citizens was pres-
ent here, in your very

capital city, on that momentous occasion
when a young Lochinvar from the West
who had dared to aspire to the salary of
one of the Potentate's postmasterships had
been placed in the arena in the midst of
an assembled multitude of Grand Dukes,
Grand Duchesses, Viziers, and Members
of Congress, and ordered to open one of

two envelopes, not knowing whether a
warrant providing him with a funeral at
the expense of the country, or a commission for a fourth-class postmastership
under a Democratic Administration, would
startle his anxious gaze. Our friend and
brother who was then present, most unfortunately found himself seated behind a
lady with a theatre bonnet of such stu-
pendous proportions upon her head, that
he was unable to see which of the two
documents the prisoner received, nor could
any but those in the front row see what
the fate of the prisoner was. Our towns-
man, who was a man of super-sensitive
feelings, was so overcome with indignation
that he fled precipitately from the arena,
and, it being in the days before the Inter-
State Commerce Act went into operation,
producing his pass, rode homeward as fast
as he could go.

" We were all very much interested in
the story which our countryman told us,
as it involved a postmastership, — than
which there is nothing dearer to the average patriotic American, — and we were
extremely sorry that he did not ask the
lady to remove her hat. We hoped, however, that in a few weeks some traveller
from your city would come among us
and bring us further news; but up to the
day upon which we left our country only
one traveller had arrived, possibly owing
to the fact that since the Inter-State Act
has come into play travellers have ceased
to arrive in Michigan, — that is, by rail.

" He, upon hearing our question, was
unable to locate the performance, saying
that from what he read in the magazines
he judged there had been several such
performances lately, adding that as theatre
hats were still in vogue, he supposed the

mystery was still as great as ever. At
last it was determined that the only thing
to be done was to send a deputation to
this country and to ask the question:
Which came forth, Death or the Postmastership?"

When the Office-Holder had heard the
mission of this highly respectable deputation, he led the visitors into the inner
office of the Bureau of Information, where
they were seated on cushions stuffed with
queries as to whether it was the Lady
or the Tiger, the Lady who smiled or the
Lady who frowned, William Bacon or
Lord Shakspeare, and various other horns
to various other dilemmas, and where, it
being Sunday in the land, lemonade, cake,
and other semi-barbaric refreshments were
served to them. Then, taking his seat
before them, the Office-Holder thus addressed the visitors: —

"Most noble strangers, before answering the question you have come so far to ask, I will relate to you an incident which occurred some years before that to which you have referred."

"His Most High Highness is going to add another story to the edifice," whispered the Chairman to his brother commissioners, touching the alarm of his repeater for the purpose of timing the narrative.

"I hope he will give us an easier one," returned the fourth commissioner, sighing deeply.

"And I hope it may be a chincapin rather than a chest —"

"It is well known," said the narrator quickly, "that in the days of King Alfred there lived a poor woman."

"It is, indeed," returned the Chairman, interrupting the Vizier in a wholly barbaric fashion, thus destroying the unities of a story relating to a semi-barbaric age. "I have read in my copy of 'Every Man His Own Historian,' that there were two poor women living in Alfred's days."

"No doubt there were," replied the narrator with a look of weariness, not relishing the interruption; "but my poor woman was a widow."

"Was this before you married her?" queried a commissioner, innocently.

"Sirrah," replied the Vice-Vizier in truly romantic fashion, "the mission of a Bureau of Information is not to answer questions. Be kind enough to confine your consumption to yon regal repast, as I am quite able to consume all the time at our command. This lady had been a woman — I should say a widow — for several years, and had but one son named Jack."

"That is not very extraordinary," whispered the Chairman. "Out in Michigan widows rarely have more than one son named Jack. In fact, it is a habit Michigan widows have, not to admit more than one Jack into a family."

"Well, I surmise you were the Jack of your family," retorted the Vizier with fine scorn. "But our Jack was no fool, although he preferred a life of elegant ease to one of toil."

"Exactly like Michigan Jacks," said the fifth commissioner, *sotto voce*, — although he would probably deny the Italian, were he confronted with it.

"Jack regularly spent the widow's income twice over," resumed the narrator, "and, in spite of his mother's constant entreaties, he would not settle down to a life other than that of a frivolous — er — frivolous — other than that of a frivolous —"

"A Frivolous Frivoler," suggested the second commissioner, seeing that the narrator was in search of the proper idiom.

"Thanks," said the Vizier, visibly relieved. "One day Jack went to market, and seeing there a large basket full of richly-colored beans, he inquired of the market-man what they were."

"'Two fra dime,' replied the affable butcher.

"'I don't mean how much are they, but what are they?' said Jack with some asperity.

"Now the butcher, knowing that Jack's extravagant nature would not admit of his buying ordinary beans, replied, —

"'That is a new vegetable; we call it *Faba vulgaris*. It goes mighty well with brown bread; and as was expected, Jack was so impressed with the rarity of the article that he purchased the whole stock. When they had been sent home, the lad, not knowing what else to do with them, constructed a bean mine in the rear garden of his mother's cottage.

"Imagine his surprise, when next morning, after a hard rain, he perceived a *Faba vulgaris* tree shooting upward toward the firmament at the rate of forty miles an

hour; and what was worse, it had taken a large part of his mother's garden with it, including the chicken-coop and pump in the spoil. This meant serious loss to Jack's unfortunate mother, and the lad was at his wit's ends to remedy the wrong of which his thoughtlessness had made him guilty. After much thought he saw that there was but one thing to do. He could not pull the stalk up — it was up far enough already. His sole chance of regaining possession of his property was to climb to the top of the tree and cut it down before it grew higher; and, being a man of impulse, Jack started."

"Who did you say was king at this time?" asked the Chairman. "Ananias?"

"Alfred, my dear sir," courteously replied the narrator. "Ananias was lying in his grave at this period."

"Ah!" was the response.

"How John managed it I do not pretend to say," said the Vizier, resuming his narrative, "but he got there just the same. A great surprise awaited him, for upon reaching the top of the tree, he discovered there a large stretch of country, which, from the fact that it had a huge granite castle built upon it, Jack knew could not have been carried up by the impetuous plant from his mother's garden. As his mother's representative,

however, the lad entered a claim for the
real estate, and proceeded to call upon
the owner of the castle, who, he learned,
was no less a person than George W.
Ogre, Esq., to suggest the propriety of his
transferring the title.

"On his way thither he was met by a
fairy, who was rather thinly dressed for
the climate at
that altitude, and
who, it seems, had
known Jack's father
when a boy, and had
supplied the butcher with
the highly-colored beans
in the hope of getting Jack up there to
call upon her. She intimated to our hero
that the Ogre was responsible for the
poverty of his mother and the death of

his father, adding that he was a man of peculiar gastronomic habits, being especially fond of *garçon croquettes à la crême.* Now Jack had always wished himself some one else, but he had no desire to become a part of the Ogre's inner man, and he at once proceeded to abscond; when, much to his terror, he saw the giant coming up the road with a basket of babies under his arm. Blinded by terror, the unfortunate boy rushed into the first house he came to, which happened to be the Ogre's residence, and fell asleep under the dining-room table."

"You don't happen to have a dining-room table handy, do you?" asked one of the commissioners, with difficulty suppressing a yawn.

The sole response was an indignant glance.

"When Jack awoke it was late at night.

He rubbed his eyes hard, and looking up through the open door into the room on the other side of thc hall, he perceived that the Ogre was experimenting with a patent hen which could lay any style of egg known to science, and a few other varieties besides, her specialty being hard-boiled nuggets.

"'That is a valuable bird,' thought Jack. 'Indeed, I never saw henything like it before. There is no law against stealing from ogres that I know of, and if the roost is to be robbed at all, I've got the right kind of a conscience to do it.'

"'Lay an egg!' said the Ogre, addressing the hen, and unconsciously interrupting Jack's moralizing.

"The hen obeyed.

"'Lay another!' said the Ogre.

"'What's that?' asked the hen. 'If

I 've got to lay a thing, I want to know what it is, first. I never saw a nother.'

" Jack with difficulty suppressed a laugh. He had never seen a really

bright hen like this before, and he was amused. Fortunately the Ogre's automatic harp began playing at this moment, and Jack's smothered smile was drowned by a variety of noises, which an etched inscription on the metal back of the harp affirmed was the song, 'What is Home without a Mortgage?' In gratitude for the service thus rendered him

Jack resolved to steal the harp too, if he could; and in order to support his new possessions in proper style, he decided likewise to remove the Ogre's gold.

"Very soon the Ogre fell asleep, and Jack, stealthily walking into the room, grabbed the bags of gold and the hen, the latter in the excitement of the abduction laying a base ball on the floor so loudly that the Ogre started from his couch and asked who was there.

"Jack very impolitely ignored the request for information, but seized the harp and ran for the door. The harp rose to the occasion by playing a double-time galop, which aroused the Ogre to a realization of the situation, and set the proper pace for Jack to keep a tolerably comfortable distance between him and his pursuer. In a short time he reached the summit of the stalk and hastily climbed down, reach-

ing his mother's garden as the Ogre started
to descend in pursuit.

.   .   .   .

"Ten minutes later the widow on walking into her back yard discovered the

giant lying dead, with the débris of the
beanstalk bestrewing his person.

" 'John,' she said, — the widow always
called her son John when she was angry
with him, — 'who killed this gentleman in
my yard and ruined the *Faba* tree?'

" 'Mother,' returned Jack, 'I can tell a

lie, but I won't. I did it with my little hatchet.'

" ' Come to my arms, my son ! ' said the happy mother, as the harp struck up, ' Truth is mighty and will prevail ; ' while the hen, in honor of the event, laid the foundations for a new cottage; 'I had rather lose all the bean-trees in Massachusetts than have a son who could n't lie.'

" It was thus," said the Deputy Vice-Vizier, rising from his seat, " that Jack, with the aid of a bushel of beans, — to drop the classics for a moment, — avenged his father, made his mother the parent of a millionnaire, and slew the Ogre.

" Now then," he continued, " when you can decide among yourselves what kind of beans those were, then will I tell you whether the gentleman your friend saw became a corpse or a postmaster."

Up to the time of going to press, the
five commissioners from the State of
Michigan had not decided.

S there is some *pericu-
lum in mora*, I beg
that you will per-
mit me to intro-
duce to you very
briefly the most
misunderstood man of the age. He has
no one but himself to blame, for

Robert B.
Rowning he
Is too much addicted t' obscuritee.

— if I may be permitted to quote what I
myself might have said in the old Biglow
days had I felt called upon to do so.

"A prize will be given to the child who after listening to the wagging of the tale can tell what tale is wagged."

The great yet obscure poet walked slowly to the edge of the platform, and holding his manuscript upside down, slowly delivered the following parleying with the muse: —

HOMO SENEX.

[The footnotes have been kindly supplied by the author of "Sardello at Home, or the Interlinear Browning."]

HE wagging of this
tale *est talis*,
It must be read *cum
grano salis;* [1]
A certain man [2] whose
cognomen I

Am not quite sure that he had any, —
Hic vir possessed a calf,

And that's one half.

Just why I do not know, —

But let that go.

'T is said he led it *ex cathedra* [3] —
The stalls were simple polyhedra [4] —
And tied it fast, yet somewhat slowly,
Unto the fence for pleasure solely [5] ;
Jam satis est — the wall

And calf make all.

Such queer arithmetic

Makes me *sic.* [6]

My poetry is quite confusing
To some ; to me it's most amusing. [7]
Rhyme can't be parsed. [8]   No English Grammar
Can break my tropes beneath its hammer.
On dit, par consequence,

I can't make sense ; [9]

Nathless I get around

The British

¹ "It must be read *cum grano salis.*" The Poet's meaning in this line is evidently that, to catch the bird of thought which is incarcerated in the cage of rhyme, the custom of old-time sportsmen of putting salt on the tail must be observed.

² The words following "A certain man" would seem to need elucidation. The poet is undoubtedly caught in a grave self-contradiction. If the hero of the poem were "a certain man," that is, a man about whom there is no uncertainty, the Poet cannot reasonably aver that concerning his cognomen he is "not quite sure." A possible explanation of the difficulty may be found in the dash following the word "any" in the fifth line

of the stanza. This may represent a hiatus, a
chasm in the manuscript, as it were, which, had
it been filled in, would have made the line as plain
as the boundless prairie. It is quite evident that
the exigencies of rhyme compelled the Poet to
make use of the hiatus ; but the reader cannot
but regret that the author did not see fit to em-
ploy an additional poetical expedient in the shape
of an asterisk and footnote, to denote what it was
that the certain man lacked.

[8] This extraordinary use of *ex cathedra* is susceptible to two explanations. If used in its
idiomatic sense of ecclesiastical authority, the expression gives some insight into the religious
training of the *Homo Senex*. A calf, to be led
from the "high seat," must have had some business there in the first place, in which case he was
undoubtedly a sacred calf, and therefore looked
up to and worshipped by the common herd. It
is impossible, however, to reconcile the idea of
the old man's ownership with that of a supremely
powerful calf, — that is to say, in heathen countries it is impossible. This being so, we are
forced, however reluctantly, to give up the notion
that the animal was a pillar of the church, and
adopt the alternative that the *cathedra* referred to
was nothing more than the ordinary milking-stool
of farm life. The commentator is well aware that
there are grave difficulties in the way of supposing
a calf to be led away from a milking-stool ; but

the reader is requested to remember that the commentator is doing the best he can with a very forlorn hope.

4 To figure to one's self a barn containing stalls which are simple *polyhedra* is a perplexing operation. It would seem natural that a sacred calf should find his dwelling-place in a polyhedronous stall; but we have already effectively disposed of the calf's claims to be regarded as above the ordinary run of heifers; and to find such an one making his home in a "many-seated" barn is surprising. The word "polyhedra," derived from πολύς and ἕδρα, is more suggestive of the theatre than the barn; yet in this very suggestion of something radically its opposite we find a plausible explanation of the Poet's words. The ancients as well as the moderns have devoted their barns on many occasions to the histrionic needs of strolling players. The term "barn-stormers" is a familiar one among the patrons of the rural stage, and there can be no reasonable doubt that the Poet in the line under discussion touchingly alludes to the days of his youth, when he attended for the first time a dramatic performance in his father's stable, doubtless deadheading his way through the secret flue connecting the humble manger of the family steed with the bins of provender above. Little glimpses like this into the boyhood days of one who is now, one might almost say, a Lar or Penate in every New England home, are surpassingly beautiful,

and cannot be held in too high estimation by the favored reader.

⁵ It may be asked, what is "a fence for pleasure solely"? Were the Poet an American boy, we might safely reply that the fence surrounding a base-ball field, chiefly constructed of knot-holes, is a fence for pleasure solely; but as the Poet is not an American, but a Briton of the deepest dye, we must confess that we cannot get over a fence of this description, and must permit the reader to browse through the field of speculation, to surmount the difficulty as to him or her seemeth best.

⁶ The Poet's use of the dead languages is very confusing. The word *sic*, employed here, can be construed to mean that the Poet is unwell or "feeling only so-so," to adopt a familiar idiom. Again, it may be that the Poet recognizes that he is addicted to confusion, and attributes his being *sic*, or thus, to the peculiar arithmetic which he finds himself compelled to work into his poem. As a precedent for this use of the word we have the line *Sic semper tyrannis*, which when translated literally means, "Tyrants are always sickly," or, "'T was ever thus with tyrants,"—referring to the condition of ill-health in which the original tyrant found himself when confronted with the person who made the remark.

⁷ This may be regarded as a much belated admission from the Poet that some of his poetry is ridiculous.

[8] "Parsed" may be a typographical error for passed. Poets frequently write phonetically, and it is quite well known that since the Author was taken up by the cultured few of our Modern Athens, he has adopted the orthoepism there prevalent. "Rhymes can't be passed" is doubtless what the poet meant to write; and we think we here detect a slight rebuke to the Chicago journal which upon a recent occasion rejected one of the Poet's odes, writing him at the same time that his work was very funny, that he showed great promise, and that he only needed to study carefully such works as "Poems of Passion," by Phœbe J. Perkins, of Peoria, Illinois, "Baled Hay," by Bill Nye, and Dr. Watts's Hymns, to fit himself for a brilliant literary future.

[9] This amounts to a confession that the Poet finds American ventures unprofitable, and is a mute appeal for an international copyright law.

[10] "Nathless I get around the British £" is a line which has greatly puzzled the commentator. The British Sovereign has, up to this writing, shown a distinct preference for another poet, one of whose effusions appears farther along in these pages; and exactly what Mr. Browning can mean by asserting that he gets around her august Majesty is not clear. It savors strongly of a vain and empty boast which is strangely unfamiliar to readers of his previous writings. An additional peculiarity to be noticed is, that the word "Sover-

eign " does not rhyme with anything that has gone before. It is greatly to be regretted that the Poet has seen fit to mar the symmetry of an otherwise exquisite sample of his work by so inartistic — and, we might add, immodest — a climax.

———

Y dear friends," said the Chairman, " it is too bad that some one better fitted for the task of present-ing the Great Eclectic Historian of Africa to you has not been chosen to preside over you this evening. My regret is all the more deep because I find myself unable to make any strikingly apt remarks concerning the gentleman I am about to introduce. I have never read his most celebrated novel, ' Ben She.' I have not even dipped into

'King Sullivan's Mines,' as I believe another well-known and favorably received
book is called. You must remember that
our African brother is a very recent addi-
tion to literature, and having inadvertently
started on a perusal of 'The Bostonians'
some three years ago, I have been unable
to find any time since to devote to other
equally valuable and more contemporaneous literary achievements.

"I trust that my friend from the Desert
will pardon this humiliating confession, and
accept my assurance that just so soon as
I can find the opportunity I shall take
great pleasure in looking through such of
his works as he may see fit to send me
If all I hear of him be true, I certainly
concur in the free translation of *Nihil teti-
git quod non ornavit*, which avers that he
touched the Nile but to adorn it."

The Reminiscencer was obviously much

embarrassed by this splendid tribute to his genius, for it was only after much persuasion that he could be induced to come forward. Finally his bashfulness was overcome, and rising from his chair he addressed the audience as follows: —

"Ladies and gentlemen, you see me at a great disadvantage this evening. I am called upon to relate to you a fairy story, when I assure you I never heard of such a thing in my life before. Most of my days have been spent fighting Boers in Africa and writing tales in England, and like that of the Distinguished Diplomat here, my reading has necessarily been limited. Up to this point it has not included anything which could be classed as a fairy story.

"However, I will do my best, and will tell you a tale which was related to me by a Zulu noble who was my valet while I was a member of the British Legation in the Transvaal. If it seem to you to be like anything you have heard before, you will please not attribute it to any plagiaristic intent on my part, but rather to coincidence to which my very minute reading has rendered me extremely susceptible. The story is called

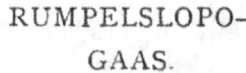

RUMPELSLOPO-
GAAS.

NCE upon a time there lived near the forest of Ku-kinikaka, in that vast district of Africa known as Nynngajakh, at the base of the snow-capped Mount Kohinoor, a poor Masai miller who had one very beautiful daughter. Her complexion was of that rich inky tint which at once betrays African blood; her hair, dressed in the prevailing style of three round woollen balls placed at intervals of three inches, beginning directly above the ear, was a shade darker than her cheek, and at night lent a deeper hue to the pall in which Nature enshrouded the land.

In her own tongue, this beautiful maiden's name was Tzukamatzatatakimeniyoshene-lephtha Twala Thumbopa;[1] but by her neighbors and friends she was familiarly known as Her.

This condensation of her baptismal appellation was largely due to the climate in which Her lived, and in which it was considered unsafe to undergo any such pro-

[1] It is very evident that names of this extensive nature were not known in the days when Shakspeare intimated that there was a dearth of matter in an appellation.

tracted effort as the pronunciation of her
name involved more than once a century.
It is perhaps not generally known that the
heat in this part of Africa is sometimes
so intense that it warps the judgment of
the natives.[1]   There is an old tradition still
preserved among them that upon one occasion, while a Masai chief was holding
friendly converse with his Zulu cousin, the
thermometer having reached an altitude of
20,000 feet above the sea-level, there was a
sudden sizzle, and 90% of the Masai evaporated and the remaining 10% of bones and
hair were shrivelled out of existence.   An
extraordinary feature of this occurrence
was that a gold watch, the bequest of a
missionary to the Zulu chief, evaporated at

---

[1] It opens up an interesting field for speculation, to
consider whether this intense heat which can warp the
judgment of man is in any way connected with the ideas
of civilized beings concerning the temperature which
is predicted for the Day of Judgment.

the same time, and was subsequently discovered in a materialized state in the
wigwam of the gentleman who had been
so unceremoniously blotted out. Considering these extraordinary climatic conditions, it is not wonderful that anything so
frail as Her's name should have succumbed,
and that the young lady should consent to
a reduction of the tax upon the articula-
tion of her friends.

Her's father was likewise in reduced circumstances. He could hardly earn enough
biltong [1] to keep himself alive, and Her had

[1] *Biltong* is a species of food much affected by the
upper classes of the Congo. It is said by those who
have eaten it and lived, to be very similar to English
sole-leather, and is supposed by some to consist of such
ingredients as gutta-percha, ivory, and lava. A cargo
submitted to an expert analytical chemist by a firm interested in its sale in this country discloses the fact that
it is harmless and nourishing, and may be left in the
hands of the young and the ignorant with impunity. The
chemist's opinion cost only $50, which is remarkable
considering the praise he accords to canned biltong,
and is likely to inspire confidence in its merits.

to go hungry on many occasions in consequence. The custom of the country
which enables millers to grow their own
hats on their own heads was a most welcome one to Thumbopa, — for such was the
miller called, — and Her's invariable habit
of making her own clothing aided materi-
ally in keeping expenses down. It is true
that when Her wanted a new dress, all she
had to do was to smile in a new way, but
it was none the less a virtue in the maiden
that she took all this upon herself. Many
of her friends in no better circumstances
could not be persuaded to do it even
to save their parents from the debtors'
prison.

Having so good a daughter was very
naturally a source of great pride to the
old miller, — of so great pride, indeed,
that he neglected his mill to brag about
her accomplishments. Among other ex-

traordinary tales he told, was one which attributed to Her the ability to turn gold into straw, an exaggeration which reached the ears of the Qing[1] and which aroused in his breast a spirit of cupidity; for you must know that straw in Central Africa is a great rarity, and is not infrequently woven into crowns for the local monarchs.

His Majesty, upon hearing of this wonderful accomplishment, sent for Her, and giving her ten nuggets of gold, commanded her to make him two bales of straw before morning, or be sacrificed to a small stucco god which formed the religious element in the royal household.

The command plunged the poor girl into the deepest distress. She had only lived twenty thousand years, and she felt it hard that she should have to die before

[1] *Qing.* —*Vide* " The Bull Roarer," Custom and Myth, by A. G'Lang.

she had attained the years of discretion.[1]
The room given her was on the ground-
floor of the palace, — which, after the manner of African palaces, was one story in
height counting the cellar, — and was stuffy
and hot. In despair Her took off the
smile she had worn in the Qing's presence,
and threw herself down by the river's brink
to think over her past life and bemoan her
fate. It was a beautiful moonlight night,
and floating along the smooth surface of
the silent river were to be seen the African
lightning-bugs, which are not very different from the bald eagle of America, and
which, when they flap their wings, emit
a sound as of a clap of thunder, and flash
forth a light which to the ordinary eye is
blinding. Altogether it was a beautiful

[1] The election laws among the Masais require a man
to be fifteen thousand years old before he votes. Masai
women are supposed to reach the years of discretion at
twenty-one thousand.

sight, — this silent river with its lightning-bugs.

Suddenly Her was awakened from her reverie by a slight rustling of the bunches of bananas on the tree before her, and be-

fore she had time to decide whether it was the wind or imagination, she was struck in the neck by a round hairy object stuck on the end of a poisoned arrow, and which transpired to be the recently decapitated head of a dog. Her sprang to her feet with an exclamation of delight, for she knew that to be hit by such an object meant that friends were near. It is one of the pleasing customs of the Masais to revive the courage of their friends in trouble by this means.

Hurriedly seizing a flat piece of wood near by, she scratched the following lines upon it : —

> " Old Mother Hubbard
>   She went to the cupboard
>   To get her poor dog a bone ;
>   But when she got there
>   The cupboard was bare,
>   And so the poor dog got none." [1]

Whether the lines were original with Her, or whether she jotted them down from memory, I cannot say. She had a habit of writing poetry in moments of intense excitement, and this may have been

[1] Compare this poem with lines in Mother Goose. The similarity is remarkable.

one of those moments for her. To the
ordinary woman it would be quite exciting
to be struck by the head of a dog at
midnight; and it is
quite likely that Her,
however extraor-
dinary her ad-
ventures may
have been,

possessed all the failings of the ordinary
woman. At all events, when she had finished, she read aloud what she had written and as the last echoes of her rich

voice died away, the withered figure of an old man crept from out the shadows of the banana-tree and stood beside her.

It was a trying moment for the girl. To be thus intruded upon at midnight when all was silent save the low rumbling roar of the lightning-bugs, even by one who bore unmistakable evidences of friendship, was no light matter for Her, especially as the moon disappeared behind a cloud at this moment. She was too terrified to speak. The words which she wished to utter froze on her lips, although the thermometer registered 106° in the shade. The man, on the other hand, seemed to wait for the lady to begin the conversation. Thus they sat until pale Luna's silver light again came forth and bathed the scene in its smiling softness. It was then and then only that Her gave a little shriek of dismay, for as the moon reappeared she remembered that she was dressed in an exceedingly *negligé* style. But here her self-possession stood her in good stead, for with an easy grace she let herself down the bank into the river until her head alone remained above the water. Then she looked inquiringly at her visitor and motioned to him to be seated on a log a few feet away.

"Good-morrow to you, lass," said the stranger.

"That all depends on how you look at it," said Her. "I'm afraid it will be a bad one for me."

"Bad, Tzukama—" began the stranger, inquiringly.

"Cut it short," interrupted Her.

"Thanks," replied the stranger, gratefully.

"Very bad," sighed the girl; "for Thumbopa, my parent, has informed the

Qing that I can turn gold into straw, and the Qing wants to put his capital into the enterprise, or sacrifice me to Saint Majolica. It is needless to say that the Miller has deviated from the dam of truth and has got me in a hole which I am quite unable to pull in after me. I can throw a rope into the air and climb up it; I can make a biltong short-cake with the next girl; and if a *rhinocodile* should bite the wheel out of the mill I'm the girl to fix it; but as for turning gold into straw I'm not *init*." [1]

"Too bad," said the old man, "but it might be worse. I've got a proposition to make that may help you out."

"Well, please to hurry up and make it, because the crocodiles are biting awfully to-night."

---

[1] Masai for inability to do something which has gone before.

" If you 'll marry me, I 'll save you."

" How old are you?"

" Ten thousand and three next February."[1]

" The idea of a boy like you wanting

to marry ! It 's absurd, and I won't do it, Mr. — er— by the way, I did n't catch your name."

" I know you did n't. I did n't throw it in your direction. However, if you

---

[1] If the stranger told the truth when he claimed to be ten thousand and three years of age, it would seem as if some official contradiction of Methuselah's claim to be the oldest man ought to be forthcoming. The Antiquarian Society should look into this matter.

won't marry me, will you give me a lock
of your hair for a bell-pull when it has
grown large enough?"

"I may lose all my hair by that time,"
pleaded Her. Her hair was one of her
strongest points, and she knew
it. She also knew that the three
knobs on the summit of the
cranium were de-
manded by Zulu

etiquette, and she did not intend to lose
her social position if she could help herself. "Besides," she added, "I never deal
in futures."

"Very well," returned the old man, rising; "if you don't promise me the knob,
you'll be dealing with a very warm future
about this time to-morrow. Give me what

I ask, and the art of turning gold into straw is yours. Deny me and —"

"I promise it, I promise it!" cried Her in despair.

"The centre knob?" demanded the stranger.

"Any one you please; but you are cruel — cruel — cru—"

There is no knowing how long Her would have cried "cruel," had not the tide risen at this moment. The Masai tides are very rapid, and have been known to rise so high in five minutes that the Qing has been compelled to adjourn the meeting of his cabinet to the top limbs of the banana-trees.

The stranger was evidently deeply moved by Her's distress, for he said that if she could guess his name within the next three days he would be willing to withdraw his claim to the lock of hair.

Then, after instructing her as to the man-
ufacture of straw from gold, and saying
Bibi, which is Zulu patois for *Au revoir*,
he disappeared into the night.

Her was greatly relieved when the
stranger had taken his departure. As she
had said, the crocodiles were unusually
vicious that night, and to make matters
worse, the tide had risen above the unhappy
girl's mouth, so that she could not even
thank the stranger for his timely succor.

Of course, now that she knew how, the
process of turning gold into straw was
comparatively easy work, and when next
morning the Qing called to collect his
first dividend, he was so pleased with the
results of Her's labors, that he asked her
to join the list of his Qeens [1] as No. 2110,
which she deemed it well to do, seeing

[1] *Qeen*, n.: The consort of the Qing. — *The Masai
Dictionary, Unabridged.*

that his Majesty left her the alternative of being fed to the elephants.

On the evening of the second day after her marriage, while the Qing was out courting a young Zulu maiden who was said to be able to make a very superior paste out of diamonds, and whom he hoped to make Mrs. Qing No. 2111, Her's mysterious benefactor called at the palace to see if the Qeen knew who he was, and to gloat over her misery.

Her, in the mean time, had had all the baptismal records of the continent since the Deluge ransacked for names; an expedition had been despatched through the subterranean passage to the Rose of Fire, near Milosis, to get such names as the tourists who had passed through had left there; the names and business addresses of all the Americans who have left their mark on the pyramids and obe-

lisks of Egypt were written down in five
large volumes; three English explorers,
who knew the way, had been sent to take
a census of the Mining District around
Kekuanaland; and the Transvaal Circulat-
ing Library had been ordered to send her
Majesty a complete, though cheap, set of
the works of Mr. Allan Quatermain, the
names of whose characters were supposed
to be as unique as anything in fiction.
Having digested all these compilations,
Her felt as well up on names, Christian
and savage, proper and improper, as if
she had been the index to the Records
which in Presbyterian circles are supposed to exist in the realms beyond.

"Ask the gentleman to *trek* [1] into the
parlor," she said to the slave who an-
nounced the visitor. Then, fixing her

---

[1] *Trek*, i. e. to tramp. It is interesting to observe
that African vagrants are known as *treks*.

hair coquettishly, so
as to make her tri-
umph over her vis-
itor all the harder
for him to bear,
and singing, " I
've got Him
on the List,"
she descend-
ed into the
parlor by
means of
an aerial
ladder,
the in-
vention
of an

African juggler, which leaned against itself, and hung suspended in the air three
feet from the floor, so as not to injure
the carpet, without making any display of

its suspenders. With an expression of triumphant joy Her greeted her guest by every name she could think of, — from Umbopa down to Ruskin, — to every one of which, to her intense dismay, he denied all claim.

When she had reached the end of her list, and he still remained a stranger in a foreign land, Her swooned away. For the first time in her life she looked above ten thousand years old. The stranger, with a heartless smirk, toyed gently with the knob on which his heart was set, and saying, " To-morrow noon will I return for thee," left the palace. The slaves carried the unhappy woman to her chamber and put her to bed.

All night long she tossed and moaned, so much so that the Qing notified her that if she tossed and moaned any more she would be used for bait at the crocodile

hunt the following week. This gentle
remonstrance had a quieting effect upon
the unhappy Qeen; but her heart was
heavy, and the tears coursed down her
cheeks, when she thought of the social

degradation to which she was doomed;
for with a single lock gone, like Samson [1]
she lost her power.

Slowly passed the night. Dawn (to be
had of all booksellers) came at last, but
with no relief for Her. At noon the thun-

[1] I got this idea of Samson out of a book called the
" Bible," published in London, 1884. — H. R. H.

derbolt must fall. No breakfast could she eat, and as a crowning misery, her hitherto loving spouse asked her if she had not made some mistake in the marriage license when she said she was born in 18200 B. C., — she looked every hour of twenty-four thousand.

After the mockery of the morning meal she seated herself at the window to watch for the coming of her persecutor. Her temples throbbed, and she nervously fingered the hour-glass, which ever and anon she would turn, and with a piece of chalk keeping tally of the hours upon the back of a slate-colored slave at her side.

As the last sand preceding mid-day passed into the lower half of the glass, she perceived the caricature of humanity who had first helped and was now endeavoring to destroy her walking toward

the palace. He was evidently very absent-minded, for he wore an old silk hat,
which he had purchased at the Cape,
around his left ankle instead of as a
bustle, which is the accepted use of the
beaver in Masai circles. He was not so
absent-minded, however, but that the lock
of the Qeen's hair was still the goal of
his ambition. He approached slowly, and
after some parley with the Kaffir at the
gate he entered the palace. A few
moments later there was a noise on the
ladder without, and the Kaffir, sticking
his head up through the floor, called
out, —

"A gent as wishes for to see Qeen 2110
is below. He says his name is Rumpelslopogaas."

"His name is what?" cried the Qeen
in astonishment, and with a little hope
springing up in her breast.

"Rumpelslopogaas," was the reply.

.   .   .   .

As before, Her dressed her hair with unusual care, and arranged her smile as became her qeenly station.   As before, she descended the aerial ladder to the audience chamber.   There was that in her eyes which boded ill for her guest as she strode past him and, mounting the throne, haughtily inquired: "Well, Rumpelslopogaas, what do you want?"

The little man nearly fainted with terror and surprise: she had the name.

"Rumpelwhatdyersay?" he screeched.

"Slopogaas, Rumpel," said the Qeen, airily.

"Spell it!" cried the visitor, beside himself with rage.

"That's not in the contract Saas, old man," retorted the Qeen with dignity, as she touched an electric button on the

arm of the throne, and so shocked her
guest that he forever after eschewed her
acquaintance.

"Good-by, Rumpel," she cried after
him as he hobbled away, tears of rage and

mortification streaming down his withered
cheek. "Next time you come, bring what
you call your mind with you, and don't
send up your name."

And the Qeen kissed her husband so
sweetly when he returned home from the

missionary hunt that evening, that he broke off the ten engagements he had con-

tracted during the afternoon, and fed all his wives except Tzukamatzatata-kimeniyoshenel-ephtha to the elephants, and the two lived happily ever after.

"OW, my dear chil-
dren," said the Dis-
tinguished Diplomat,
" I want you to pay
the greatest attention
to what is to follow.
My good friend who is about to address
you is a very great singer; not, I beg you
to believe, in the sense that a *prima donna*
is a great singer, for no letter in a known
alphabet could be set as a limit to the
height of his notes—and I may parenthet-
ically remark, by way of encouragement
to such young poets as may be in this
audience, that he has frequently soared as

8

high as a five-pound note while in the service of my good friend the Empress of India. For many years he sang the praises of his noble land, — a land which will always be a *terra firma* in the affections of your humble servant, — a land whose greatness is largely due to the good fortune it had *laudari a viro laudato*, and who has since been made a Laud on account of it.

"During my ministry at the Court of St. James, I remember seeing him oftentimes sitting in the Poet's corner writing verses at the command of Her Most Gracious Majesty Queen Victoria. Always ready, *nunquam non paratus*, whatever his subject; a living paradox, Baron yet fertile, Lord yet subject, Peer yet Poet, in the seedtime yet budding still, we shall now have the pleasure of listening to the pearls of poesie as they drop from the lips of this great Oyster of song, — if my noble friend will pardon my carrying the metaphor to its logical conclusion."

After a salvo of applause the Poet-Peer wrapped his robes about him, removed the coronet from his brow, and with a majestic tread walked to the footlights and sonorously delivered the following lines : —

CINDERELLA.

HILDREN, leave me here a little ; I, who am no longer young, Find it difficult to put my musings in a modern tongue.

'T is some threescore years since first I twanged
    the harp in Locksley Hall,
And it 's fortunate for you, dears, that I get around
    at all.

I am not so good of hearing, and my eyes are
    not so sharp
As they were when England echoed every tinkle
    of my harp.

But my voice is still the voice that once evoked
    a poet's fame,
And if I'm a trifle senile I shall get there just
    the same.

Time has streaked with silver whiteness all my
    wealth of raven hair ;
Time is money, — specie payment, — and it finds
    resumption there.

Yet for every hair of silver, in my heart there is a
    rhyme,
And I'll string a few together if you'll only give
    me time.

I will loop them all together, I will string them in
    a chain
For a garland, little children ; listen well and
    I'll explain, —

Listen well unto the story which the Laureate
 shall sing,
Full of love as is the trysting of two bluebirds in
 the Spring.

In the Spring a little madder tints the temper of
 the rose ;
In the Spring a young man's fondness is for
 anything but prose ;

In the Spring a maiden's bonnet shows the iris
 of the wren ;
In the Spring the budding poet is addicted to
 the pen.

So I, too, in life's sweet springtime, when the
 Idyls all were done,
Wrote this fairy-tale so famous, just for exercise
 and fun.

Then her cheek was round and rosy as should
 be in any case,
And her conversation seemed to me the height
 of verbal grace.

And I said, "My Cin-
derella, on the rosary
of truth,
Backward tell the beads,
that I may learn the
story of your youth."

On her cheek the blushes
hinted of the rose's
pinky leaf,
In her eye the moisture
gathered in the storm-
cloud of her grief;

And she turned northeast
by north, and in a
most dramatic style
Struck the keynote of her sorrow and the sunshine of her smile,

Saying, "I have laved the linen for a family of
three ; "
Saying, "That was long ago, but now they get
no more of me."

Here she took a glass of water in her jewel-
  fingered fist ;
Every second as she swallowed irrevocably was
  missed.

Then, refreshed, proceeded slowly, and with very
  great detail,
To repeat the little story of the slipper small and
  frail.

You 'll excuse me if I tell it in my own peculiar
  way,
For her grammar had the errors of the grammars
  of her day.

Now I think as all the points of the defence are
  handed in,
It is time that I the counsel for the plaintiff should
  begin.

Cinderella had two sisters, — the relationship
  was such
That they weren't disposed to congregate together very much.

History records precisely, and
    the little lass avers,
That her father was their
    father, but their mother
    was n't hers.

Jealousy the seeds of
    Hatred sowed

                            in Cinder-
                            ella's home ;
When her sisters brushed her hair they never
    failed to yank the comb.

Cinderella's beauty brought her bitter blossom-
    ings of Hate,
And her goings were restricted by the kitchen
    and the gate.

She was slave to their siestas when the dinner
    hour was o'er ;
She must wash the china dishes, she must scrub
    the kitchen floor ;

She must shovel coal, and Monday do the wash-
    ing in the morn ;
She must wear a constant smile that shall but
    sharpen up their scorn ;

She must sleep up in the garret, say her prayers
    a prey to rats,
And avoid a chance of comfort on a bedstead
    minus slats.

They would call her naughty names and do their
    best to make her say
Something wrong to give their mother's muscle
    exercise that day.

But her feelings, lignum-vitæ, though they suf-
    fered, she controlled,
And the silver of their speeches she returned with
    silence, gold.

Now it chanced a handsome Prince had sent
    some invitations out
For a german, which excited all the neighborhood
    about.

To this ball the hateful sisters of dear Cinderella
    went,
Happy in their miser hearts, and in her pain and
    discontent.

And they taunted her when going, saying, " Don't
    you wish that you
Were a lady like your sisters, and with them were
    going too ? "

" Mock me not," quoth Cinderella ; " life has
    other joys for me.
I shall keep myself from mischief darning stock-
    ings after tea."

Scarcely had their figures vanished ere beside the chim-
ney-breast
Came the sound as of a
breathless and a much-
belated guest ;

And a voice of
strange falsetto
smote the unof-
fending air ;
And it murmured,
"Cinderella,
Cinderella, are
you there ? "

So excited was
the maiden in
her dark, de-
serted home,
That she spoke before she knew it, and articu-
lated, "Gnome ! "

"It is I, the same," the stranger said, assuming
mortal guise,

"'T is thy god-greetest standing thine eyes.　mother thou here before

"Hist thee, Know ye the hour Hie thee　Cinderella ! that 't is now of nine ; straight into the garden, — snatch a pumpkin off the vine."

With her wondrous wand the stranger touched the sympathetic gourd : Lo ! it changed into a carriage like aris-tocrats afford.

"Hist thee, Cinderella ! Hither bring the mouse-
　　trap and the mice,
And the latter shall be neatly metamorphosed in
　　a trice."

With her wondrous wand the stranger touched
    the left, anon the right;
Lo! they changed into four horses, — two of
    black and two of white.

"Hist thee, Cinderella! Hie thee to the garret
    dark and dim;
Fetch me here a roving rodent, for I have a
    need of him!"

With her wondrous wand she touched him, saying
    something very weird:
Lo! he changed into a coachman with a uniform
    and beard.

Then to Cinderella spake she in a language quaint
    and queer :
Lo ! she found herself in satins, with a diamond
    in each ear.

In a wink her graceful figure was arrayed in fine
    brocade,

And she noticed
that the boxes all
were C. O. D.,
and paid.

But of all the trinkets
pretty which so
pleased the little
lass

Was a pair of dainty slippers numbered one and
    made of glass.

" Hist thee, Cinderella ! Drive ye to the palace
    of the King,

But be sure that you
're at home before
the midnight hour
shall ring."

Then the Gnome went up the chimney whence
she came a moment since,
And dear Cinderella hastened to the german and
the Prince.

All the noble lords and ladies paused and
 courtesied to her
As she swept the polished marbles, where her
 scornful sisters were.

And the Prince her "Dancing Order" quite
 monopolized, and she
Was the picture of his fancy, it was plain enough
 to see.

And he pledged her in the rarest and the most
expensive wines,
Till his eyes were traitors to him, and all zigzag
were his lines.

So she triumphed at the german over all the
guests, until
It was rumored that her sisters found the evening
very chill.

Yet I doubt not through the ages one pervading
    purpose runs,
And the eyes of girls are dazzled by the brilliance
    of the sons.

Oh, the evening was so pleasant, and the ices were
    so good,
It was hard for her to leave them as she prom-
    ised that she would.

So she tarried, and the Prince began his pastoral
    of love,
And she quite forgot the midnight till the clock
    struck quarter of.

Up she jumped, and from the palace in a storm
    of girlish fear
Scorned decorum, rushing onward like a hunted,
    frightened deer.

And she never slacked her speed until she reached
    the house, and there
When she added up her slippers found she had
    but half a pair.

Sleep for her was very broken. Things for her
were in a fix ;
And a worried conscience called her in the morning long ere six.

Hark ! the King's policemen shouting in the middle of the street ;
They are crying, " Cinderella, what 's the measure
of your feet ? "

They had tried to fit that slipper for a dreary,
dreary while,
And the feet that they had measured were enough
to make a mile.

But when Cinderella took it and with great as-
    surance put
The extraordinary slipper on her pretty little
    foot,

They exclaimed, " Behold a Princess ! " for the
    Prince had made an oath
That this slipper was so precious he was bound
    to have them both.

"And the lady who can wear them," quoth the
    Prince, "upon my life,
I will marry ere the sundown, and to-day shall
    be my wife."

So the Prince and Cinderella wedded on the sixth
    of May,
And lived happily together, so the scornful sisters
    say.

And the sisters begged her pardon, and she did
    the handsome thing,
And secured for them positions as domestics for
    the King.

Howsoever these things be, a long farewell, fare-
    well to all ;
Sixty years is quite an absence, — I must on to
    Locksley Hall.

Comes a look within your faces like a diamond in
    the rough,
And it leads me to imagine that you all have had
    enough.

So I bid you all good-evening, — and it has been
    good, I know ;
Time is growing quite impatient, roaring me-ward,
    and I go.

THE
GREAT ROMANCER IS FIT-
TINGLY INTRODUCED.

———

Y dear children," said
the Chairman, "you
all know that ex-
quisite line from a
literature which,
though written
in a language
long called dead, is yet undying, — *Finis
coronat opus.*

"Wisely has the Great Romancer *qui
exegit monumentum aere perennius* been
asked to preside over the end which
crowns the work ; and the distinguished
gentleman who sat at the other end must

not think that I am making invidious
comparisons, or saying aught to hurt his
feelings, when I assert that it is at this
end that the coronation takes place. He
said an infinitely harder thing of himself
when he told the world that all the stories have been told, apparently forgetting
that he still remained to idealize the real
for us, while the Great Romancer, whom
we are now to hear, had just begun to
realize the ideal.

"My romantic friend will superintend
the oscillation of the narrative of Beauty
and the Beast, — a story which from the
days of my youth I have regarded as *fa-
cile princeps* in fairy literature. It is a
story which — " here the Distinguished
Diplomat became embarrassed. He had
lost the manuscripts pertaining to the
whichness of the story; and after a moment's hesitation he cleared his throat and

added, " But I trespass on your time, and taking a hint from the immortal Spanish bard, who sang

> Hablen cartas
> y callen barbas, —

' Let writings speak, and beards be silent,' — I will ask our modern Pacha of many tales to lead us into the twilight that surrounds the borderland of old Romance."

The readings were then brought to a close by the Great Romancer, whose manuscript ran as follows : —

THE STRANGE CASE OF BEAUTY AND THE BEAST.

I.

THE INCIDENT OF THE ROSE.

R. TUTTERSON the mer-
chant was a man of
a rugged countenance
that was never lighted
by a smile, unfortunate
in business, lengthy,
lank, and yet lovable
as the possessor of a
beautiful daughter. When everything went
well with him, there was something about
him that inspired confidence which even
his fondness for himself could not overcome; but when angry, Mr. Tutterson,

without making any perceptible effort, could be as mad as the next man.

The chief pleasure which Mr. Tutterson derived from life, independent of the olive branch which adorned his household, came from a habit of rambling through the streets on Sunday afternoons, plucking flowers from the miniature parks, and wishing he knew of some island wherein there lay hidden the fabulous treasures of long-forgotten pirates.

It chanced in one of his Sunday afternoon rambles that his way led him down a by-street in an almost uninhabited quarter of London. The street was small, and on either side were the gardens of the occupants of the one or two villas which had been erected in the neighborhood. Within the largest of these gardens Mr. Tutterson perceived a bush on which were growing several magnificent specimens of the cabbage-rose. Beyond the bush was a sinister-looking house in whose windows the shades were pulled tightly down. Mr. Tutterson did not perceive that beneath one of the shades there peered a pair of the most malignant-looking eyes conceivable. Had he done so, he never would have ventured to open the gate stealthily and walk on tiptoe to where the roses were growing.

He was a prudent man, was Mr. Tutterson, and he would much rather have gone to a florist and purchased the flowers which he had promised to take to his daughter, than purloin the blossoms of others when their owner was around to see him do it.

It was growing dark rapidly as Mr. Tutterson drew near the bush. It may have been for this reason that he did not see the knob of the grim-looking door

turn slowly as he reached out to pick the
largest flower from its stem.   In another
instant the rose was picked, and Mr.
Tutterson became dimly conscious that
he had been struck by an avalanche or
some such overwhelming mass.   As he
said when in after years he related the
occurrence to his grandchildren, he felt as
if the sinister-looking mansion before him
had fallen upon him.   Always direct in
his speech, he cried out, " Help ! Help ! "

Then to his terror he saw before him a
form so utterly horrible and depraved in
appearance as to surpass belief.   It was
not the house that had fallen upon Mr.
Tutterson; it was the genius of the house,
the owner of the roses, and the essentially
sinful-looking being which he saw before
him that had dropped into his life, whence
he knew not.

Again Mr. Tutterson cried, " Help ! "

"Help!" retorted the fiendish proprietor with a satanic smile. "What do you want help for? Seems to me you're able to help yourself!" pointing to the rose which

Mr. Tutterson still held in his nerveless grasp.

"What's the good of falling on a man from the third-story window of a sinister-looking building just because of a cabbage-rose!" asked Mr. Tutterson, rubbing the back of his neck.

"I didn't fall from the third-story

window; I jumped from the roof of the veranda. It is a regular Sunday afternoon pastime of mine, and if you were in the way it was your own fault. I didn't ask you to cabbage my roses."

"Let me go!" cried Mr. Tutterson, angrily.

"I will not only let you go, but I will assist you in the movement," retorted the Beast; for that the fiend was a beast Mr. Tutterson was convinced. True to his word was Mr. Tutterson's new acquaintance; and when next the merchant had recovered his scattered faculties, he was on the other side of the street, while about him played the shadows of the sinister-looking building with the drawn blinds, bent but not broken, the cabbage-rose that he had plucked still adorning his buttonhole, where he had placed it during his parley with the Beast.

As for the latter, he had disappeared.

II.

MR. TUTTERSON'S DECISION.

THAT evening Mr. Tutterson came home
in sombre spirits, and ate his dinner without seating himself at table. It was his
custom of a Sunday, when this meal was
over, to sit by the fire until twelve, and

then go soberly and gratefully to bed. On this night, however, he felt as if he had had all the fire he could stand for one day, and could not find it compatible with the remedies he took to ameliorate his sufferings, to go to bed quite so soberly as usual. Before retiring he called his daughter to him and related the incident of the rose to her, taking the flower from his buttonhole and twirling it nervously while he spoke.

Beauty — as Mr. Tutterson called his daughter — was very indignant at the treatment her father had received, and wished to take the rose back, " before another hour had rung out from the minster on the hill." Of this, Mr. Tutterson would not hear, saying that he would send the Beast a check for ten shillings the next morning to pay for the rose, and would then sue him for ten pounds' damages to his feelings as soon as he could get around again.

Mr. Tutterson then wearily sought his couch, and, as befitted his tired state, slept soundly until long after the birds began their morning carol in the trees.

The next morning, in accordance with a settled plan, Beauty set off to carry the ten shillings to the Beast, and to serve a summons of complaint upon him for assault and battery.

III.

THE TUTTERSON ELOPEMENT.

AFTER his daughter had gone out, Mr. Tutterson lay wearily down upon his bed and nursed his wounded vanity and his wrath. Never before had he been so treated. How disproportionate to the value of the rose was the chastisement he had received at the hands of the Beast! Was ten pounds sufficient compensation for the loss of self-respect to which being thrown bodily across the public highway subjected a man, to say nothing of the assaulting and battering he had received before he crossed the highway?

From his soul Mr. Tutterson wished he had instituted suit for £20.

"If I could collect a shilling on each pound I received from that depraved inhabitant of the sinister-looking building, I'd get £40," he whispered sadly to his dog which lay whining at his side.

Musing thus, Mr. Tutterson sat until the luncheon-hour, when his appetite warned him of the flight of time. His daughter had not returned, and Mr. Tutterson began to grow anxious.

"The Beast surely would not treat a lady as he treated me," he thought; "still, a Beast who would treat any one as he treated me on such short acquaintance would do anything!"

As the morning went, so passed the afternoon; still, Beauty did not return.

The shadows of night crept across the threshold, and Mr. Tutterson began to lose his temper. He was growing very hungry, and as his daughter combined with her beauties of person the duties of cook, Mr. Tutterson did not see exactly where his evening meal was coming from.

The moaning cry of the newsboy could be heard far down the street, but save this all was silent. Alone the merchant sat, starting nervously betimes when he thought he heard a footstep upon the porch. The ticking of the clock upon the mantel grew momentarily more pronounced, and every swing of the pendulum but added to the dyspeptic overflow which was gradually welling up in Mr. Tutterson's breast. Instead of "tick-tock, tick-tock," it seemed to say, "Tut-terson, Tut-terson, what have you done, what have you done?" until the lonely man was in a condition of mind bordering on insanity.

Fortunately for the clock, — for Mr. Tut-terson had reached for his boot to throw at the dial, — as the hour-hand pointed to half after six, and the minute-hand was loitering in the neighborhood of a quarter to seven, there came a loud knock at the front door.

The sick man started, and craning his neck until his Adam's apple seemed like the apex to a pyramid, he gazed into the darkness of the hall-way as if afraid to believe in the reality of the sound. He tried to cry out, "Who's there?" but the apple stood in his way and he simply gurgled.

Again the knock came, and following it was a scarcely muffled curse against the sinfulness of people who keep messenger- boys standing out in the rain; for it

was raining hard without.

"Come in," cried Mr. Tutterson.

"The door is bolted," cried the mes- senger, for it was he.

The word "bolted" filled Mr. Tutterson with blank dismay. Not only did
it account for his dyspepsia, but it was
a possible explanation of Beauty's absence.

Forgetting his pain, Mr. Tutterson
sprang to the door and opened it. The
messenger thrust into his hand a small
envelope, the inscription so blurred that
Mr. Tutterson hardly recognized himself
as the person addressed. With a white
face the merchant broke the seal. The
letter read : —

SEPTEMBER 1.

MY DEAR FATHER, — I called at the Beast's
this morning, and found him so exceedingly
handsome and agreeable that I decided to become Mrs. Beast. It was a great deal cheaper,
dear father, than paying ten shillings for a paltry
rose, and lawsuits for damages are quite as
damaging to the damagee as to the damagor.
When Mr. B. and I return from our wedding

tour, we will give ourselves the pleasure of calling upon you.

Your affectionate daughter,

BEAUTY TUTTERSON BEAST.

P. S. There is some cold chicken in the kitchen closet, *dear* father.

B. T. B.

If the messenger had chosen to look back at the door he had just left, he would have seen an old man lying prone upon the porch, with a damp, crumpled note clasped tightly in his left hand.

Mr. Tutterson had fainted from hunger.

IV.

THE SEARCH FOR THE BEAST.

THERE is no knowing how long Mr. Tutterson would have remained in a swoon, had not a leak in the piazza roof caused the water to drop on his wan, white face. The leak revived him.

Starting to his feet, he rushed madly into the house, threw open the pantry door, clutched the deli- cate viands which Beau- ty's postscript told him were there, and ravenously consumed them. His pangs of hunger sat- isfied, Mr. Tutterson gained new strength. He resolved to seek out his daughter and rescue her, for he had fully made up his mind that the letter had been written under restraint. The first

part of Beauty's letter, it seemed to Mr.
Tutterson, was lacking in the exuberant
affection which the inedited letters of
daughters usually betray, and there were
no italics; and Mr. Tutterson was sufficiently familiar with the literary habits of
womankind to know that, had the letter
been spontaneous, so glaring an omission
would have been impossible. On the
other hand, the sorrowing parent thought
the postscript showed that the thought-
fulness which had ever characterized
Beauty's relations with her father still
remained; and the next to the last word
was italicised. Mr. Tutterson's theory,
based upon a comparison of the body of
the letter with the postscript, was that the
first part had been dictated to the unhappy girl by her abductor, while the
postscript was influenced by the dictates
of her own heart; and the lonely father

thought he could read between the lines
a mute appeal to him to come to his
daughter's assistance at once.

With Mr. Tutterson, to resolve was to
do. It took him but three minutes to
fortify himself for the approaching strug-
gle, and armed with his family umbrella
he set forth. In a very brief space of
time he arrived before the sinister-looking
mansion. It was a great relief to Mr.
Tutterson to find it still there, although
now that he stood before it and observed
by the street-lamp's dim light that the
window-shades were still pulled tightly
down, his anxiety to penetrate within its
doors abated considerably.

"To go or not to go, that is the question," said Mr. Tutterson, whose familiarity with Shakspeare enabled him to adapt
the phrases of the great dramatist to any
occasion. "I would n't hesitate a moment

if these pavements were a little softer," he added reminiscently.

Then the possibility that his daughter was suffering flashed across his mind, and he hesitated no longer. He unlatched the gate, and with a bold front marched up the garden walk. This time he scanned every nook and corner of the house as if dreading to discover the malignant eye of the Beast. His heart beating wildly, he rang the bell, whose sound had barely died away before the door was opened, and the Beast, holding a rattan stick in his hand, stood before him.

Mr. Tutterson gulped convulsively. A second view of the repulsive creature confronting him convinced him that Beauty had become Mrs. Beast against her own free will.

"Marry that creature from choice? Pshaw! the idea is absurd," thought Mr. Tutterson.

" Well? " said the Beast, impatiently.

" Not quite," returned Mr. Tutterson. " But somewhat better, thank you," he added politely. It was just as well, he thought, to be diplomatic.

" No repartee, if you please," retorted the Beast, angrily. " I don't care for tea in any shape — much less repartee. What are you doing on my stoop? "

" I seek my daughter," replied the merchant with dignity.

" Well, you 're doing your seeking in the wrong neighborhood. If she is where she daughter be, she 's at home, and I 'll allow you four seconds to start in that direction yourself. I thought I gave you to understand the other day that there was no room for your kind around here? "

" You certainly gave me that among other more or less painful impressions," cried Mr. Tutterson ; " but a father's place is by his daughter's side, and I intend to get there if I die for it. Restore her to me or take the consequences. I'll have you up for incendiarism, or whatever the crime is."

"Oh, you will, eh?" retorted the Beast, getting red in the face and swishing the rattan through the air. "Well, if it is incendiarism to fire a man off my premises, incendiarism is just the crime I am about to stain my soul with. Come!"

And then Mr. Tutterson repeated his gymnastic feat of the Sunday afternoon previous. The door of the sinister-looking mansion slammed to; the Beast disappeared, swallowed up in the blackness of his retreat, and Beauty still remained a prisoner.

"Heavens!" roared Mr. Tutterson, the analogy being suggested by the extreme prevalence of stars in his neighborhood.

" To think that Beauty *could* bring herself
to marry that wretch, and say that he is
lovely, amiable, and handsome, even if her
refusal imperilled her life! However,"
he added, as if the thought comforted
him, " if she is like her grandmother on
her mother's side, perhaps she 'll tame
him."

With these remarks Mr. Tutterson
dragged himself slowly and painfully
home.

V.

MR. TUTTERSON MAKES A DISCOVERY.

As he drew near his own house Mr.
Tutterson was surprised to see a light
burning in his parlor. He had left no
one in the house, and the unexpected
illumination filled his soul with alarm.
"Who can it be?" he asked himself over

and over again. Burglars would surely
not rob his house, for they had entered
it so often before to find nothing, that Mr.
Tutterson could have slept with his doors
and windows open, and never have been
troubled except by an occasional tramp
who wished for a place to sleep.

His physical condition precluded his
contending with the invaders of his household alone and unaided; so before entering his hall he called to him one of his
neighbors, a stout, well-built fellow, who,
Mr. Tutterson thought, could stand up
before even the Beast without serious dam-
age to his personality. To his neighbor
Mr. Tutterson confided his fears, and the
two men walked into the house together
prepared to wreak vengeance on the in-
truders. As they entered, a few chords
were struck on the piano in the merchant's
parlor, and much to the old man's delight

the voice of his beloved daughter was raised in a song dear to his memory.

"She has escaped, thank Heaven!" cried the merchant, with tears of joy running down his cheeks. "Beauty, here is papa!" he added, throwing open the parlor door.

"Why, where have you been?" asked Beauty, as if her father's absence was the one thing in the world that needed explanation. "We have been quite worried about you."

At the word *we*, Mr. Tutterson looked faint.

"We?" he asked. "Who is we?"

"Why, Mr. Beast and I. We took a wedding tour down to the British Museum, and then came right home."

"Is that man in my house?" asked the father, sternly.

"Yes, father, and I know you will like him, he is *so* handsome and kind."

"Handsome and kind!" shrieked Mr. Tutterson, rising and getting behind his neighbor. "Handsome may be in the use of his hands, and kind of a certain kind, but not my kind. Why, he 's homely enough to stop a train!"

"You do him wrong, dear papa. Charlie would n't stop a train, I know," returned the simple girl. "Just wait till you see him; he 's upstairs now, putting on a clean collar."

"Oh, indeed! Well, perhaps *my* turn has come, we will proceed to see my charming, kind, amiable son-in-law, who has hitherto amused himself by propelling his father-in-law across the street. Perhaps the collaring we give him won't suit his style of neck. If you happen to hear a dull thud in the back yard, don't get excited; and to-morrow you may buy yourself a crêpe veil and other emblems of mourning. The funeral will be from his late residence. Come along, neighbor; I have work for you above."

With these words Mr. Tutterson seized his neighbor by the arm, and pushing him before him rushed up stairs. Beauty remained below, fearing to witness the tragedy which she fully expected would now ensue. The irate Mr. Tutterson, with more noise and bravery than was usual with him, rushed from room to room in search of his prey, until at last, standing before a looking-glass adjusting his tie, he found him. A cry of amazement was all that Beauty, waiting tearfully in the parlor, could hear; then she heard her father's voice calling to her to come up-stairs. Like a dutiful daughter she obeyed, and on entering the room she perceived the merchant seated on the bed, his mouth wide open, while before him stood a handsome, graceful young man who looked rather sheepish and nervous.

"Beauty," said Mr. Tutterson, "who is this, I'd like to know?"

"My husband, papa dear," replied Beauty with a bright smile.

"Are you Mr. Beast?" demanded Mr. Tutterson of the blushing youth.

"Th–th–that's my n–n–name, sir."

"Do you live in a sinister-looking mansion on the Duke of Westminster Lane, S. W., London?"

"A house with the window-shades pulled tightly down?" queried the youth.

"The same," ejaculated Mr. Tutterson.

"That's my residence, dear father-in-law," was the simpering response.

"Well, what Dr. Jekyll business have we struck, anyhow? This afternoon you were a roaring, red-eyed, snub-nosed, shock-headed dwarf, with a temper like a bull and a fist like a battering-ram; and to-night you are a sweet-tempered, mild-mannered, lady-like youth. How do you account for it, anyhow?"

VI.

THE SON-IN-LAW'S EXPLANATION.

"I FAWNCY you must have seen my father."

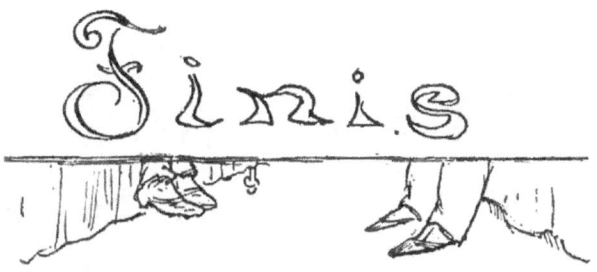

A LIST OF BOOKS

PUBLISHED BY

TICKNOR AND COMPANY,

BOSTON.

Full-faced type indicates books published since January, 1886.

. For Forthcoming and Latest Books, see Page 23.

AMERICAN-ACTOR SERIES (The). Edited by Lau-
rence Hutton. A series of 12mo volumes by the best writers, embracing
the lives of the most famous and popular American Actors. Illustrated.
Six volumes in three. Sold only in sets. Per set, $5.00.

    Vol. I. Edwin Forrest. By Lawrence Barrett. The Jeffersons. By
      William Winter.
    Vol. II. The Elder and the Younger Booth. By Mrs. Asia Booth Clarke.
      Charlotte Cushman. By Clara Erskine Clement.
    Vol. III. Mrs. Duff. By Joseph N. Ireland. Fechter. By Kate Field.
      Also a limited edition on large paper, especially adapted to the use of
    collectors and bibliophiles, for extending, etc. 6 vols. Per vol., $5.00

AMERICAN ARCHITECT. See back cover page.

AMERICAN WHIST. See Whist.

ARNOLD'S (Edwin) The Light of Asia. Beautiful illustrated edition. 8vo. $6.00. In antique morocco, or tree-calf, $10.00.

———————— (George) Poems. Edited, with a Biographi-
cal Sketch of the Poet, by William Winter. With Portrait. 16mo. $1.50.
Half-calf, $3.00. Morocco antique or tree-calf, $4.00.

AUSTIN'S (Jane G.) A Nameless Nobleman. A Novel.
1 vol. 16mo. Eighteenth edition. $1.00. In Ticknor's Paper Series, 50 cents.

———————— The Desmond Hundred. A Novel. 16mo.
$1.00. In paper covers, 50 cents.

AUSTIN'S (JANE G.) Nantucket Scraps ; Being Experiences of an Off-Islander, in Season and out of Season, among a Passing People. 16mo. $1.50.

BACON'S (HENRY) Parisian Art and Artists. 8vo. Profusely illustrated. $3.00.

BALLOU'S (MATURIN M.) **Due North.** 1 vol. 12mo. $1 50.

————Genius in Sunshine and Shadow. 1 vol. 12mo. $1.50.

———— **Edge-Tools of Speech.** 1 vol. 8vo. $3.50. Sheep, $5.00. Half-calf or half-morocco, $6.50.

BARTLETT'S (TRUMAN H.) The Art-Life of William Rimmer. With Illustrations after his Paintings, Drawings, and Sculptures. 4to. Full gilt. $10.00.

BATES'S (ARLO) Patty's Perversities. A Novel. 1 vol. 16mo. $1.00. In Ticknor's Paper Series, 50 cents.

BELLAMY'S (EDWARD) Miss Ludington's Sister. $1.25. In Ticknor's Paper Series, 50 cents.

BENJAMIN'S (S. G. W.) **Persia and the Persians.** 1 vol. 8vo. With Portrait and many Illustrations. Beautifully bound. $5.00. Half-calf, $9.00.

———— (MRS. S. G. W.) **The Sunny Side of Shadow:** Reveries of a Convalescent. 1 vol. 16mo. $1.00.

BENT'S (SAMUEL ARTHUR) Familiar Short Sayings of Great Men. 8vo. $3.00. Half-calf, $5.50. New and cheaper edition. Fifth edition, revised and augmented. 12mo. $2 00.

BIRD'S-EYE VIEW OF THE WORLD, A. See page 14.

BOIT'S (ROBERT APTHORP) Eustis. 12mo. $1.50.

BOSTON, Memorial History of. See page 30.

BOWDOIN COLLEGE. See CLEAVELAND.

BROOKS'S (HENRY M.) **The Olden-Time Series.** Each vol. 16mo. 50 cents. The six volumes, in a neat box, $3.00.
  I.   Curiosities of the Old Lottery.
  II. Days of The Spinning-Wheel in New England.
  III. New-England Sunday.
  IV. Quaint and Curious Advertisements.
  V.   Some Strange and Curious Punishments.
  VI. Literary Curiosities.

BROWN'S (FRANCES CLIFFORD) **A Stroll with Keats.** 1 vol. Square 16mo. Richly illustrated. $1.50.

———— (HELEN DAWES) **Two College Girls.** 12mo. $1.50.

———— (SUSAN ANNA) The Invalid's Tea-Tray. Illuminated boards. 50 cents.

BROWN'S (Susan Anna) How the Ends Met. 12mo.
50 cents.
———— In Bridget's Vacation. Leaflets to hang up.
50 cents. On gilt bar and rings. 75 cents.

BROWNING'S (Mrs. Elizabeth Barrett) **Sonnets from the Portuguese.** Illustrated by Ludvig Sandöe Ipsen. 1 vol.
Oblong folio. Beautifully bound. Gilt top. $15.00. In full tree-calf, $30.00.
The unrivalled gift-book of the year.

BUDDHIST RECORDS OF THE WESTERN WORLD.
Translated from the original Chinese, with Introduction, Index, etc. By
Samuel Beal, Trinity College, Cambridge. 2 vols. 12mo. $7.00.

BUDGE'S (Ernest A.) The History of Esarhaddon (Son of Sennacherib), King of Assyria, B.C. 681-668. From Cuneiform Inscriptions. 8vo. Gilt top. $4.00.

BUNNER'S (H. C.) A Woman of Honor. 16mo. $1.25.

BURNHAM'S (Clara Louise) **Next Door.** 12mo. $1.50.

BUSH'S (James S.) The Evidence of Faith. 12mo. $2.00.

BYNNER'S (Edwin Lassetter) **Agnes Surriage.** A
Romance of Colonial Massachusetts. 12mo. $1.50.
———— **Penelope's Suitors.** 1 vol. 24mo. Quaintly
bound. 50 cents.
———— Damen's Ghost. A Novel. 1 vol. 16mo.
$1.00. In paper covers, 50 cents.

BYRON'S (Lord) Childe Harold. A sumptuous new illustrated edition. In box. $6.00. In antique morocco, padded calf, or tree-calf, $10.00. In crushed Levant, with silk linings, $25.00.

———— **Childe Harold. Tremont Edition.** 1 vol. 16mo.
Beautifully illustrated. With red lines and gilt edges. $2.50. Half-calf,
$4.00. Antique morocco, tree-calf, flexible calf, or seal, $5.00.
———— **Childe Harold. Pocket Edition.** 1 vol. Little-
Classic size. Many Illustrations. Elegantly bound. $1.00. Half-calf,
$2.25. Antique morocco, flexible calf, or seal, $3.00. Tree-calf or padded
calf, $3.50.
———— **Childe Harold. Students' Edition.** Edited, with
Notes and Introduction, by W. J. Rolfe. 12mo. Illustrated. 75 cents.

CARLYLE (Thomas) and *RALPH WALDO EMERSON,* The Correspondence of. Edited by Charles Eliot Norton. 2 vols.
12mo. Gilt tops and rough edges. With new Portraits. $4.00. Half-
calf, $8.00. Half-morocco, gilt top, uncut edges, $8.00. New Library
Edition, $3.00 ; in half-calf, $6.00.
New revised edition with 100 *pages of newly-found letters.*

———— Supplementary Volume, including the newly-
found letters. 16mo. $1.00.

CAROLINO'S (Pedro) New Guide of the Conversation
in Portuguese and English. First American edition. With an Introduction by Mark Twain. 16mo. $1.00. Paper, 50 cents.

CARPENTER'S (Henry Bernard) **Liber Amoris;**
Being the Book of Love of Brother Aurelius. A Metrical Romaunt of the
Middle Ages. 16mo. Gilt top and rough edges. $1.75.

CARRYL'S (Charles E.) Davy and the Goblin. 1 vol.
8vo. Fully illustrated. $1.50.

CESNOLA'S (Gen. L. P. di) The Cesnola Collection of
Cyprus Antiquities. A Descriptive and Pictorial Atlas. Large folio. 500
Plates. *Sold by subscription only.* Send for Prospectus.

CHAMBERLAIN'S (Basil Hall) The Classical Poetry
of the Japanese. 8vo. $3.00.

CHAMPNEY'S (Mrs. L. W.) Rosemary and Rue. A
Novel. 1 vol. 16mo. $1.00. In paper covers, 50 cents.

CHASE'S (Miss E. B.) Over the Border. 1 vol. 12mo.
Illustrated with Heliotype Engravings from Original Drawings of Scenery
in Nova Scotia. With Map. 12mo. Third edition. $1.50.

CHENOWETH'S (Mrs. C. van D.) Stories of the Saints.
Illustrated. 12mo. $2.00.

CLARK'S (T. M.) Building Superintendence. 8vo. With
Plans, etc. $3.00.

CLARKE'S (Rev. James Freeman) **Every-Day Religion.**
1 vol. 12mo. $1.50.

———————— Events and Epochs in Religious History.
Crown 8vo. Illustrated. $3.00. Half-calf, $5.50.
New and cheaper edition. 12mo. $2.00.

———————— The Ideas of the Apostle Paul. 12mo. $1.50.

———————— Self-Culture. Thirteenth edition. 12mo. $1.50.
Half-calf, $3.00.

CLEAVELAND'S (Nehemiah) and *PACKARD'S* (Alpheus Spring) History of Bowdoin College. With Biographical Sketches
of its Graduates, from 1806 to 1879, inclusive. With many full-page Por-
traits, and other Illustrations. 8vo. $5.00.

CLEMENT'S (Clara Erskine) and *CONWAY'S*
(Katherine E.) Christian Symbols and Stories of the Saints.
1 vol. Large 12mo. With many full-page Illustrations. $2.50. Half-calf,
$5.00.

———————— Stories of Art and Artists. 1 vol. 8vo.
Profusely Illustrated. $4.00. Half white vellum cloth, $4.50.

———————— and *HUTTON'S* (Laurence) Artists of the
Nineteenth Century. 12mo. Fully revised up to 1885. $3.00. Half-
calf, $5.00. Tree-calf, $7.00.

———————— A Handbook of Legendary and Mythological
Art. Eighteenth edition. 12mo. $3.00. Half-calf, $5.00. Tree-calf, $7.00.

———————— Painters, Sculptors, Architects, Engravers, and
their Works. Illustrated profusely. Ninth edition. 12mo. $3.00. Half-
calf, $5.00. Tree-calf, $7.00.

CLEMENT'S (CLARA ERSKINE) Eleanor Maitland. A
Novel. 16mo. $1.25. In Ticknor's Paper Series, 50 cents.

CLEMMER'S (MARY) Poems of Life and Nature. $1.50.

——————— **Men, Women, and Things.** Revised and
Augmented. 12mo. $1.50.

——————— **His Two Wives.** 12mo. $1.50.

——————— **Memorial Biography. An American Woman's Life and Work.** By EDMUND HUDSON. 1 vol. 12mo. With
Portrait. $1.50.

COLLIER'S (ROBERT LAIRD) English Home Life. 16mo.
Gilt top. $1.00

COLLING'S (J. K.) Art Foliage. Entirely new plates
from the latest enlarged London edition. Folio. $10.00.

CONWAY'S (M. D.) Emerson at Home and Abroad. $1.50.

COOKE'S (GEORGE WILLIS) George Eliot ; A Critical
Study of her Life, Writings, and Philosophy. 12mo. With Portrait. $2.00.
Half-calf, $4.00.

——————— Ralph Waldo Emerson ; His Life, Writings, and
Philosophy. 12mo. With Portrait. $2.00. Half-calf, $4.00.

——————— **Poets and Problems.** Tennyson, Ruskin, Browning. 12mo. $2.00.

——————— (JOHN ESTEN) Fanchette. A Novel. 1 vol.
16mo. $1.00. In paper covers, 50 cents.

——————— (MRS. LAURA S. H.) Dimple Dopp. Small
4to. Illustrated. $1.25.

——————— (MRS. ROSE TERRY) **Happy Dodd.** 12mo. $1.50.

——————— Somebody's Neighbors. 12mo. Fourth edition.
$1.50. Half-calf, $3.00.

——————— **The Sphinx's Children.** 12mo. $1.50.

CRADDOCK'S (CHARLES EGBERT) Where the Battle
Was Fought. A Novel. 12mo. Fourth edition. $1.50.

CROWNINSHIELD'S (FREDERIC) **Mural Painting.**
1 vol. Square 8vo. With numerous full-page Illustrations. $3.00.

CUNNINGHAM'S (FRANK H.) Familiar Sketches of the
Phillips Exeter Academy and Surroundings. Illustrated. $2.50.

DAHLGREN'S (MRS. MADELEINE VINTON) A Washington
Winter. 12mo. $1.50.

——————— **Lights and Shadows of a Life.** A
Novel. 1 vol. 12mo. $1.50.

——————— **The Lost Name.** A Novelette. 1 vol.
16mo. $1.00.

——————— Memoir of John A. Dahlgren, Rear-Admiral
U. S. Navy. 8vo. With Portrait and Illustrations. $3.00.

DAHLGREN'S (Mrs. Madeleine Vinton) South-Sea
Sketches. 12mo. $1.50.
——————— South-Mountain Magic. 12mo. $1.50.
DANENHOWER'S (Lieut. J. W.) Narrative of the
Jeannette. Paper covers. 25 cents.
DOBSON'S (Austin) Thomas Bewick and his Pupils.
With numerous Illustrations. Crown 8vo. $3.50. Limited large-paper
edition. $10.00.
DODGE'S (Theodore Ayrault, U.S.A.) A Bird's-Eye
View of our Civil War. 1 vol. 8vo. With Maps and Illustrations. $3.00.
——————— The Campaign of Chancellorsville. 8vo. $3.00.
EASTWICK'S (Edward B., F.R.S., M.R.A.S.) The Gulis-
tan; or, Rose Garden of Shekh Mushlin'ddin Sâdi. 8vo. $3.50.
EATON'S (D. Cady) Handbook of Greek and Roman
Sculpture. Second edition, revised and enlarged. 12mo. $2.00.
Pocket edition, for travellers. 16mo. 415 pages. $1.00.
EDMUNDSON'S (George) Milton and Vondel. A Curi-
osity of Literature. 1 vol. Crown 8vo. $2.50.
EMERSON, The Genius and Character of. A Series of
Lectures delivered at the Concord School of Philosophy, by eminent
authors and critics. Edited by F. B. Sanborn. Illustrated. 12mo. $2.00.
EMERSON–CARLYLE CORRESPONDENCE (The).
See Carlyle.
EMERSON'S (Mrs. Ellen Russell) Myths of the In-
dians; or, Legends, Traditions, and Symbols of the Aborigines of America.
8vo. Gilt top. With numerous Plates and Diagrams. $5.00.
FAVORITE–AUTHORS SERIES. Favorite Authors,
Household Friends, Good Company. Three volumes in one. Illustrated.
8vo. Full gilt. $3.50.
FAWCETT'S (Edgar) **The Confessions of Claud.**
12mo. $1.50.
——————— **The House at High Bridge.** 12mo. $1.50.
In Ticknor's Paper Series, 50 cents.
——————— Social Silhouettes. 12mo. $1.50.
——————— The Adventures of a Widow. 12mo. $1.50.
——————— Tinkling Cymbals. A Novel. 12mo. $1.50.
——————— Song and Story. A Volume of Poems. $1.50.
——————— **Romance and Revery.** A Volume of
Poems. 12mo. Fine laid paper. Rough edges. $1.50.
FEATHERMAN'S (A.) The Aramæans; Social History
of the Races of Mankind. 8vo. Uncut edges, gilt top. $5.00.
——————— **The Nigritians.** Division One of the
Social History of the Races of Mankind. 1 vol. 8vo. $6.00.
——————— **The Melanesians.** Division Two of
the Social History of the Races of Mankind. 1 vol. 8vo. $6.00.

FENOLLOSA'S (ERNEST F.) Review of the Chapter on
Painting in Gonse's " *L'Art Japonais.*" 12mo. Paper covers. 25 cents.

FIELD'S (EUGENE) **Culture's Garland**: Being Memoranda
of the Gradual Rise of Literature, Art, Music, and Society in Chicago and
other Western Ganglia. 12mo. Cloth. $1.00. In Ticknor's Paper
Series, 50 cents.

FOOTE'S (MRS. MARY HALLOCK) The Led-Horse Claim.
A Novel. Illustrated by the Author. 16mo. $1.25.

———— **John Bodewin's Testimony**. A Novel. 12mo.
$1.50

FRITH'S (I.) **The Life and Works of Giordano Bruno.**
8vo. With Portrait. $4.50.

FROMENTIN (EUGÈNE): Painter and Writer. From the
French of Louis Gonse, by Mrs. MARY C. ROBBINS. 8vo. Illustrated. $3.00.

FROMENTIN'S (EUGÈNE) The Old Masters of Belgium
and Holland. 8vo. With eight full-page Heliotypes. Translated by Mrs.
MARY C. ROBBINS. $3.00.

FULLER'S (ALBERT W.) **Artistic Homes in City and
Country.** Fourth edition. Oblong folio. 76 full-page Illustrations.
$4.50.

GARDNER'S (E. C.) Homes and all about them. 3 vols.
in 1. Profusely illustrated. 12mo. $2.50.

GARFIELD (PRESIDENT JAMES ABRAM) The Works of.
Edited by BURKE A. HINSDALE. 2 vols. 8vo. With new Steel Portraits.
$6.00. Sheep, $8.50. Half-morocco or half-calf, $10.00.
Edition de luxe. 2 vols. 8vo. $25.00. *Sold by subscription only.*

GAYARRE'S (CHARLES) Aubert Dubayet. 12mo. $2.00.

GERALDINE: A Souvenir of the St. Lawrence. A Poetical Romance. 16mo. Ninth edition. $1 25. Half-calf, $3.00. In Ticknor's Paper Series, 50 cents.

GOETHE, The Life and Genius of. Concord Lectures for
1885. Edited by F. B. SANBORN and W. T. HARRIS. With Portraits. $2.00.

GOETHE'S Faust. Translated by A. Hayward. $1.25.

GRANT'S (ROBERT) An Average Man. 12mo. $1.50.

———— The Confessions of a Frivolous Girl. $1.25. In
Ticknor's Paper Series, 50 cents.

———— The Knave of Hearts. $1.25.

———— **A Romantic Young Lady.** 1 vol. 12mo. $1.50.

GREENOUGH'S (HORATIO) **Letters to his Brother,
Henry Greenough.** With biographical sketches and some contemporary correspondence. Edited by FRANCES BOOTT GREENOUGH. 1 vol.
12mo. With portrait. $1.25.

———— (MRS. RICHARD) **Mary Magdalene**; a
Poem. 12mo $1 50.

GREENOUGH'S (Mrs. Richard) **Mary Magdalene, and Other Poems.** With photograph of Greenough's statue of Mary Magdalene on the cover. 50 cents.

GRÉVILLE'S (Henry) **Cleopatra.** A Russian Romance. 1 vol. 16mo. With portrait of the author. $1.25.

———————— Dosia's Daughter. 16mo. $1.25.

———————— **Count Xavier.** 16mo. $1.00.

HALE'S (Lucretia P.) **The Peterkin Papers.** New and copiously illustrated Holiday Edition of 1886. 8vo. $1.50.

HAMILTON'S (Kate W.) Rachel's Share of the Road. 1 vol. 16mo. $1.00. In paper covers, 50 cents.

HAMLIN'S (Augustus C.) Leisure Hours among the Gems. Illustrated. 12mo. $2.00.

HAMMOND'S (Mrs. E. M.) The Georgians. 1 vol. 16mo. $1.00. In paper covers, 50 cents.

HARRIS'S (Joel Chandler) Mingo, and other Sketches in Black and White. 16mo. $1.25.

———————— Nights with Uncle Remus. Illustrated. $1.50. In paper covers, 50 cents.

HARTING'S (James Edmund, F.L.S., F.Z.S.) British Animals Extinct within Historic Times. With some Account of British Wild White Cattle. Illustrated. 8vo. Gilt top. $4.50.

HARTT'S (Professor C. F.) Geology and Physical Geography of Brazil. *In preparation.*

HASSARD'S (J. R. G.) A Pickwickian Pilgrimage. $1.00.

HATTON'S (Joseph) Henry Irving's Impressions of America. 1 vol. 12mo. $1.50.

HAWTHORNE'S (Julian) Nathaniel Hawthorne and his Wife. A Biography. With New Portraits on Steel, and Etched Vignettes. 2 vols. 12mo. $5.00. Half-morocco or half-calf, $9 00. Edition de luxe. $15.00. New Library Edition, $3.00; in half-calf, $6.00.

———————— **Confessions and Criticisms.** A Volume of Essays and Reminiscences. 12mo. With Portrait. $1 25.

———————— Love — or a Name. 12mo. $1.50.

———————— Beatrix Randolph. 12mo. $1.50.

———————— Fortune's Fool. 12mo. $1.50.

———————— (Nathaniel) Dr. Grimshawe's Secret. 12mo. $1.50. Library edition. Gilt top. $2.00.

HAYES'S (Henry) **The Story of Margaret Kent.** $1.50. In Ticknor's Paper Series, 50 cents.

———————— Sons and Daughters. 12mo. $1.50.

HAYWARD'S (ALMIRA L.) The Illustrated Birthday
Book of American Poets. Revised and enlarged edition, with index for
names, and portraits of thirteen great American poets. 1 vol. 18mo. $1.00.
Half-calf, $2.25. Flexible morocco, seal, or calf, $2.50.

HAZEN'S (GEN. W. B) A Narrative of Military Service.
8vo. With Maps, Plans, and Illustrations. $3.00.

HEARN'S (LAFCADIO) Stray Leaves from Strange Litera-
ture. Stories reconstructed from the Anvari-Soheili, Baitál-Pachisi, Ma-
habharata, Gulistan, etc. 1 vol. 16mo. $1.50.

HENDERSON'S (ISAAC) **The Prelate.** A Novel. 1 vol.
12mo. $1.50. In Ticknor's Paper Series, 50 cents.

HINSDALE'S (BURKE A.) President Garfield and Educa-
tion. Portraits of Gen. Garfield, Mrs. Garfield, etc. 12mo. $1.50. Half-
calf, $3.00. Morocco antique, $4.00.

——————— Schools and Studies. 16mo. $1.50.

HOME-BOOK OF ART (THE). Heliotype Plates after
One Hundred Classical and Popular Pictures by the most famous Artists of
the World. With descriptions. Twenty-five parts at one dollar each. Or
all bound in 1 vol. Cloth, $28.00. Half-morocco, $31.00. Full morocco,
$33.00. *By subscription only.*

HOME SANITATION. A Manual for Housekeepers.
1 vol. 16mo. 50 cents.

HOSMER'S (G. W.) The People and Politics. 8vo. $3.00.

HOWARD'S (BLANCHE W.) Aulnay Tower. 12mo. $1.50.

——————— Aunt Serena. A Novel. 16mo. Sixteenth
edition. $1.25.

——————— Guenn. 12mo. Twenty-third edition. $1.50.
In Ticknor's Paper Series, 50 cents.

HOWE'S (E. W.) The Mystery of the Locks. 12mo. $1.50.

——————— The Story of a Country Town. 12mo. Seventh
edition. $1.50. In Ticknor's Paper Series, 50 cents.

——————— **A Moonlight Boy.** 1 vol. 12mo. With Portrait
of the author. $1.50.

HOWELLS'S (W. D.) **The Minister's Charge.** 12mo. $1.50.

——————— Tuscan Cities. With many fine Illustrations
by Joseph Pennell. Richly bound, full gilt edges, in box, $5.00. In
tree-calf, or antique morocco, $10.00.

——————— **Indian Summer.** 12mo. $1.50.

——————— The Rise of Silas Lapham. 12mo. $1.50.

——————— A Fearful Responsibility. 12mo. $1.50.

——————— A Modern Instance. 12mo. $1.50. In
Ticknor's Paper Series, 50 cents.

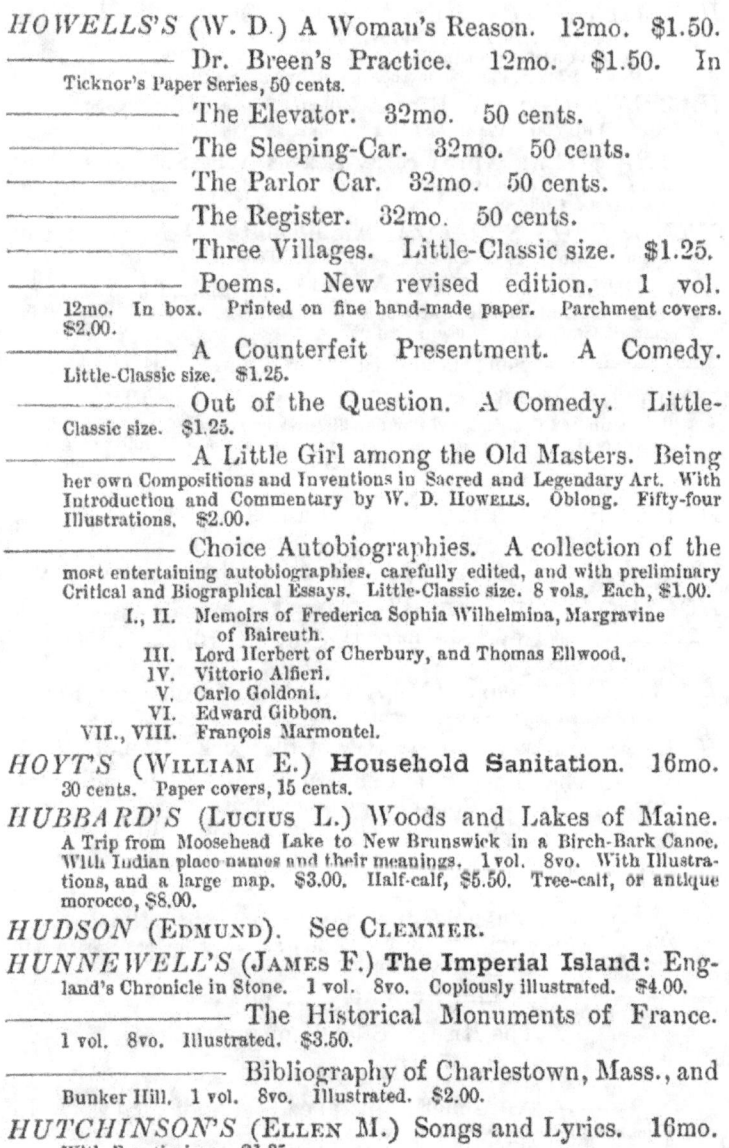

HOWELLS'S (W. D.) A Woman's Reason. 12mo. $1.50.

———————— Dr. Breen's Practice. 12mo. $1.50. In Ticknor's Paper Series, 50 cents.

———————— The Elevator. 32mo. 50 cents.

———————— The Sleeping-Car. 32mo. 50 cents.

———————— The Parlor Car. 32mo. 50 cents.

———————— The Register. 32mo. 50 cents.

———————— Three Villages. Little-Classic size. $1.25.

———————— Poems. New revised edition. 1 vol. 12mo. In box. Printed on fine hand-made paper. Parchment covers. $2.00.

———————— A Counterfeit Presentment. A Comedy. Little-Classic size. $1.25.

———————— Out of the Question. A Comedy. Little-Classic size. $1.25.

———————— A Little Girl among the Old Masters. Being her own Compositions and Inventions in Sacred and Legendary Art. With Introduction and Commentary by W. D. HOWELLS. Oblong. Fifty-four Illustrations. $2.00.

———————— Choice Autobiographies. A collection of the most entertaining autobiographies, carefully edited, and with preliminary Critical and Biographical Essays. Little-Classic size. 8 vols. Each, $1.00.

   I., II. Memoirs of Frederica Sophia Wilhelmina, Margravine of Baireuth.
    III. Lord Herbert of Cherbury, and Thomas Ellwood.
    IV. Vittorio Alfieri.
    V. Carlo Goldoni.
    VI. Edward Gibbon.
  VII., VIII. François Marmontel.

HOYT'S (WILLIAM E.) **Household Sanitation.** 16mo. 30 cents. Paper covers, 15 cents.

HUBBARD'S (LUCIUS L.) Woods and Lakes of Maine. A Trip from Moosehead Lake to New Brunswick in a Birch-Bark Canoe. With Indian place-names and their meanings. 1 vol. 8vo. With Illustrations, and a large map. $3.00. Half-calf, $5.50. Tree-calf, or antique morocco, $8.00.

HUDSON (EDMUND). See CLEMMER.

HUNNEWELL'S (JAMES F.) **The Imperial Island:** England's Chronicle in Stone. 1 vol. 8vo. Copiously illustrated. $4.00.

———————— The Historical Monuments of France. 1 vol. 8vo. Illustrated. $3.50.

———————— Bibliography of Charlestown, Mass., and Bunker Hill. 1 vol. 8vo. Illustrated. $2.00.

HUTCHINSON'S (ELLEN M.) Songs and Lyrics. 16mo. With Frontispiece. $1.25.

HUTTON'S (LAURENCE) Literary Landmarks of London.
1 vol. 12mo. $1.50.

IRVING (HENRY) See HATTON.

JAMES (HENRY, SR.), The Literary Remains of. Edited by WILLIAM JAMES. 1 vol. 12mo. With Portrait. $2.00.

JAMES'S (HENRY) The Author of Beltraffio ; Pandora ;
Georgina's Reasons ; The Path of Duty ; Four Meetings. 12mo. $1.50.

———— The Siege of London ; The Pension Beaurepas ;
and The Point of View. 12mo. $1.50.

———— Tales of Three Cities (The Impressions of a
Cousin ; Lady Barberina ; A New-England Winter). 12mo. $1.50. In Ticknor's Paper Series, 50 cents.

———— A Little Tour in France. 12mo. $1.50.

———— Portraits of Places. 12mo. $1.50.

———— Daisy Miller : A Comedy. 12mo. $1.50.

JOHNSON'S (ROSSITER) Idler and Poet. 16mo. $1.25.

———— (VIRGINIA W.) **The House of the Musi-
cian.** 1 vol. 16mo. In cloth. $1.00. In Ticknor's Paper Series, 50 cents.

JOHNSTON'S (ELIZABETH BRYANT) Original Portraits
of Washington. Sixty Portraits, from paintings, sculptures, etc. With descriptive text. 1 vol. 4to. $15.00. Half-morocco, $20.00. *By subscription only.*

KEATS. See BROWN (F. C.).

KEENE'S (CHARLES) Our People. Four Hundred Pictures from *Punch.* 4to. $5.00.

KENDRICK'S (PROFESSOR A. C.) Our Poetical Favorites.
Three volumes in one. Illustrated. 8vo. Full gilt. $3.50.

KING'S (CLARENCE) Mountaineering in the Sierra Nevada.
12mo. With Maps. Eighth edition. $2.00.

———— (EDWARD) The Golden Spike. 12mo. $1.50.

———— The Gentle Savage. 12mo. $2.00.

KIRK'S (MRS. ELLEN OLNEY) A Midsummer Madness.
A Novel. 1 vol. 16mo. $1.25.

———— A Lesson in Love. 1 vol. 16mo. $1.00. In
paper covers, 50 cents.

LEOPARDI'S (G.) Essays and Dialogues. 8vo. $3.00.

LIEBER, The Life and Letters of Francis. Edited by
THOMAS SERGEANT PERRY. 8vo. With Portrait. $3.00. Half-calf, $5.50.

LIGHT ON THE HIDDEN WAY. With Introduction
by JAMES FREEMAN CLARKE. 1 vol. 16mo. $1.00.

LINCOLN'S (Mrs. Jeanie Gould) Her Washington
Season. A Novel. 12mo. $1.50.

LONGFELLOW'S (Samuel) **Life of Henry Wadsworth**
Longfellow. With extracts from his Journals and Correspondence.
Crown 8vo. 2 vols. With Steel Portraits, Engravings on wood, fac-similes,
etc. $6.00 ; half-calf, with marbled edges, $11.00 ; half-morocco, with gilt
top and rough edges, $11.00.

———————————— **Final Memorials of Henry Wads-**
worth Longfellow. 1 vol. 8vo. Uniform with the "Life." With
two new steel plates, and other illustrations, $3 00. Half-calf or half-
morocco, $5.50. Limited large-paper edition, numbered copies, $7.50.

LOWELL'S (Percival) Chosön: The Land of the Morn-
ing Calm. A Sketch of Korea. 1 vol. 8vo. Illustrated. $5.00. In half-
calf, $9.00. In tree-calf, $12.00.

MACHIAVELLI (Niccolo), The Historical, Political,
and Diplomatic Works of. Translated by Christian E. Detmold. 4 vols.
8vo, with Steel Frontispieces, in a box. $15.00. Half-calf, $30.00.

MADAME LUCAS. Vol. VIII. of the Round-Robin Series of novels. 16mo. $1.00. In paper covers, 50 cents.

MADDEN'S (F. W.) The Coins of the Jews. 4to. $12.00.

MATTHEWS. See Sheridan.

MEREDITH'S (Owen) Lucile, Illustrated. Holiday Edi-
tion. With 160 new Illustrations. Elegantly bound, with full gilt edges,
in box, $6.00. Tree-calf, flexible calf, or antique morocco, $10.00. Spanish
calf, $11.00. Crushed levant, silk linings, $25.00.

———————————— Lucile. Tremont Edition. 1 vol. 16mo.
Beautifully illustrated. With red lines and gilt edges, $2.50. Half-calf,
$4.00. Antique morocco, tree-calf, flexible calf, or flexible seal, $5.00.

———————————— Lucile. Pocket Edition. 1 vol. Little-
Classic size. Thirty Illustrations. Elegantly bound, $1.00. Half-calf, $2.25.
Antique morocco, flexible calf, or seal, $3.00. Tree-calf or padded calf, $3.50.

MONOGRAPHS OF AMERICAN ARCHITECTURE,
No. 1. Harvard Law School. H. H. Richardson, architect. 18 Plates
(Gelatine, from nature), 13 × 16 In portfolio. $5.00.

No. 2. **The State Capitol, at Hartford, Conn.** Richard M.
Upjohn, architect. 22 Plates (Gelatine, from nature), 13 × 16. $6.00.

No. 3. **The Ames Memorial Buildings at North Easton,**
Mass. H. H. Richardson, architect 22 Gelatine Plates (from nature),
13 × 16 inches. Also two Lithographs. In portfolio. $6.00.

No. 4. **The Memorial Hall at Harvard University.**
Ware & Van Brunt, architects. 13 Gelatine Plates (from nature), 13 × 16
inches. Also one Photo-lithograph. In portfolio. $5.00.

MONTAUBAN'S (G. De) **The Cruise of a Woman**
Hater. 16mo. Cloth. $1.00. In Ticknor's Paper Series, 50 cents.

MONTI'S (Luigi) Leone. A Novel. 1 vol. 16mo. $1.00.
In paper covers, 50 cents.

MORRILL'S (Hon. Justin S.) **Self-Consciousness of** Noted Persons. 8vo. $1.50.

MORSE'S (Edward S., Ph.D.) Japanese Homes and their Surroundings. 8vo. With 300 Illustrations. $5.00; half-calf, $9.00.

NEKRASOV'S (N. A.) **Red-Nosed Frost.** Translated in the original metres from the Russian. With the Russian Text. 1 vol. 16mo. With Portrait. $1.50.

NELSON'S (Henry L.) John Rantoul. 12mo. $1.50.

NORTON'S (Gen. C. B.) American Inventions in Breechloading Small Arms, Heavy Ordnance, etc. 4to. 250 Engravings. $10.00.

OLDEN-TIME SERIES. See Brooks.

OPERETTA IN PROFILE, AN. By Czeika. 1 vol. 16mo. $1.00.

OSGOOD'S GUIDE-BOOKS. See Ticknor.

OWEN'S (William Miller) In Camp and Battle with the Washington Artillery of New Orleans. Illustrated with Maps and Engravings. 1 vol. 8vo. $3.00.

PALFREY'S (John Gorham) A Compendious History of New England. 4 vols. 12mo. With new Index. In a box. $6.00. Half-calf, $12.00.

PEIRCE'S (Mrs. Melusina Fay) Co-operative Housekeeping. Square 16mo. 60 cents.

PENINSULAR CAMPAIGN (The) of General McClellan in 1862. (Vol. I., Papers of the Military Historical Society of Massachusetts.) 8vo. With Maps. $3.00.

PEPPERMINT PERKINS, The Familiar Letters of. Illustrated. 16mo. $1.00. In paper covers, 50 cents.

PERRY'S (Nora) For a Woman. 16mo. $1.00.

——— A Book of Love Stories. 16mo. $1.00.

——— The Tragedy of the Unexpected. 16mo. $1.25.

——— **New Songs and Ballads.** 12mo. $1.50.

——— After the Ball, Her Lover's Friend, and other Poems. Two volumes in one. $1.75.

——— (Thomas Sergeant) **The Evolution of the** Snob. 16mo. $1.00.

——— From Opitz to Lessing. 1 vol. 16mo. $1.25.

PHILIPS'S (Melville) **The Devil's Hat.** A Novel. 1 vol. 16mo. $1.00.

PICTURESQUE SKETCHES. Statues, Monuments, Fountains, Cathedrals, Towers, etc. 1 vol. Oblong folio. $1.50.

PLYMPTON'S (Miss A. G.) The Glad Year Round.
Square 8vo. $2.50.

POETS AND ETCHERS. Twenty full-page etchings, by
James D. Smillie, Samuel Colman, A. F. Bellows, H. Farrer, R. Swain Gifford, illustrating poems by Longfellow, Whittier, Bryant, Aldrich, etc.
4to. $10.00.

POOLE'S (W. F., LL.D.) An Index to Periodical Literature. 1 vol. Royal 8vo. $15.00. Sheep, $17.00. Half-morocco, $18.00.
Half-morocco, extra, gilt top, uncut edges, $19.00.

PORTER'S (Robert P.) Protection and Free Trade To-Day: At Home and Abroad. 16mo. Paper covers. 10 cents.

PREBLE'S (Admiral George H.) History of the Flag
of the United States of America, etc. Third Revised Edition. 240 Illustrations, many of them in colors. 1 vol. Royal quarto. $7.50.

PRESTON'S (Miss H. W.) The Georgics of Vergil. 18mo. $1.

———————— The Georgics of Vergil. Holiday Edition.
Four full-page Illustrations. 1 vol. Small 4to. Full gilt. $2.00.

PUTNAM'S (J. Pickering) The Open Fire-Place in all
Ages. With 300 Illustrations, 53 full-page. 12mo. $4.00.

———————— Lectures on the Principles of House Drainage.
With Plates and Diagrams. 16mo. 75 cents.

QUINCY'S (Edmund) The Haunted Adjutant; and other
Stories. Edited by his son, Edmund Quincy. 1 vol. 12mo. $1.50.

———————— Wensley; and other Stories. Edited by his
son, Edmund Quincy. 1 vol. 12mo. $1.50.

RECLUS'S (Onésime) A Bird's-Eye View of the World.
A popular scientific description of the great natural divisions of the globe, their lakes, rivers, mountains, and other physical features, and their political divisions; and of the peoples that inhabit them, their growth, distinctive characteristics, languages, and religions; with descriptions and populations of all the principal cities. In one beautiful royal octavo volume of 936 pages. With 400 illustrations. *Sold by subscription only. Send for prospectus.*

REVEREND IDOL (A). A Novel. 12mo. Twelfth
edition. $1.50. In Ticknor's Paper Series, 50 cents.

RICHARDSON'S (Abby Sage) Abelard and Heloise.
1 vol. Little-Classic size. $1.00.

———————— Old Love-Letters; or, Letters of Sentiment. Written by persons eminent in English Literature and History.
1 vol. Little-Classic size. $1.25.

ROBINSON'S (Edith) Forced Acquaintances. A Novel.
12mo. $1.50.

ROCHE'S (James Jeffrey) Songs and Satires. $1.00.

ROCKHILL'S (W. WOODVILLE) The Life of the Buddha,
and the Early History of his Order. 1 vol. 12mo. Gilt top. $3.00.

ROLFE'S (W. J.) Students' Series of Standard Poetry,
Edited, with Notes and Introductions, by W. J. ROLFE. Each in 1 vol.
12mo. Beautifully Illustrated. 75 cents.

Byron's **Childe Harold.**	**Young People's Tennyson.**
Scott's Marmion.	Select Poems of Tennyson.
Scott's The Lady of the Lake.	**The Lay of the Last Minstrel.**
Tennyson's The Princess.	**Enoch Arden, and Other Poems.**

ROUND-ROBIN SERIES (THE). A series of original
novels by the best writers. Each is complete in 1 vol. 16mo. $1.00.
Also, new popular edition, in paper covers, each, 50 cents.

A Nameless Nobleman.	A Tallahassee Girl.
A Lesson in Love.	Dorothea.
The Georgians.	The Desmond Hundred.
Patty's Perversities.	Leone.
Homoselle.	Doctor Ben.
Damen's Ghost.	Rachel's Share of the Road.
Rosemary and Rue.	Fanchette.
Madame Lucas.	His Second Campaign.

The Strike in the B —— Mill.

SADI'S GULISTAN. See EASTWICK.

SANBORN'S (KATE) A Year of Sunshine. Comprising
cheerful selections for every day in the year. 1 vol. 16mo. $1.00.

———————— Grandma's Garden. Leaflets, with illuminated covers. $1.25.

———————— Purple and Gold. Choice Poems. Leaflets,
with illuminated covers by ROSINA EMMET. $1.25.

———————— Round-Table Series of Literature Lessons.
Printed separately on sheets. Twenty-five authors. Price for each author,
enclosed in envelope, 25 cents.

———————— (F. B.). See EMERSON, also GOETHE.

SANGSTER'S (MARGARET E.) Poems of the Household.
1 vol. 16mo. $1.50.

SCHIEFNER'S (PROFESSOR) Tibetan Tales. Translated
by W. R. S. RALSTON, M.A. $5.00.

SCHOPENHAUER'S (ARTHUR) **The World as Will and
Idea.** Translated from the German by R. B. HALDANE, M.A., and JOHN
KEMP, M.A. 3 vols. 8vo. $5.00 a vol.

SCOTT"S (SIR WALTER) **The Lay of the Last Minstrel.**
Holiday Edition of 1886-87. 1 vol. 8vo. In neat box. With over 100
new Illustrations by famous artists. Full gilt edges. Elegant binding.
$6 00. Flexible or tree calf, or antique morocco, $10.00. Crushed levant,
with silk linings, $25.00.

———————— **The Lay of the Last Minstrel.** Tremont
Edition. 1 vol. 16mo. Beautifully illustrated. With red lines, bevelled
boards and gilt edges, $2.50. Half-calf, $4 00. Tree-calf, antique morocco,
flexible calf, or seal, $5.00.

SCOTT''S (SIR WALTER) **The Lay of the Last Minstrel.**
Pocket Edition. 1 vol. Little-Classic size. With thirty illustrations.
Elegantly bound, $1.00. Half-calf, $2.25. Antique morocco, flexible calf,
or seal, $3.00. Tree-calf, or padded calf, $3.50.

———— **The Lay of the Last Minstrel.** Students'
Edition. Edited, with Notes and Introduction, by W. J. ROLFE. 12mo.
Illustrated. 75 cents.

———— Marmion. Holiday Edition. Over 100 new
Illustrations by famous artists. Elegantly bound. Full gilt edges. In
box, $6.00. Tree-calf, flexible calf, or antique morocco, $10.00. Crushed
levant, with silk linings, $25.00.

———— Marmion. Tremont Edition. 1 vol. 16mo.
Beautifully illustrated. With red lines, bevelled boards, and gilt edges,
$2.50. Half-calf, $4.00. Antique morocco, flexible calf, flexible seal, or
tree-calf, $5.00.

———— Marmion. Pocket Edition. 1 vol. Little-Classic
size. With thirty Illustrations. Elegantly bound, $1.00. Half-calf,
$2.25. Antique morocco, flexible calf, or seal, $3.00. Tree-calf, or padded
calf, $3.50.

———— Marmion. Students' Edition. Edited, with
Notes and Introduction, by W. J. ROLFE. 12mo. Illustrated. 75 cents.

———— The Lady of the Lake. Holiday Edition. 1 vol.
8vo. In box. 120 Illustrations. $6.00. Tree-calf, flexible calf, or antique
morocco, $10.00. Crushed levant, with silk linings, $25.00.

———— The Lady of the Lake. Tremont Edition. 16mo.
Beautifully illustrated. Red lines. $2.50. Half-calf, $4.00. Tree-calf,
antique morocco, flexible calf, or flexible seal, $5.00.

———— The Lady of the Lake. Pocket Edition. 1 vol.
Little-Classic size. 30 Illustrations. $1.00. Half-calf, $2.25. Antique
morocco, flexible calf, or seal, $3.00. Tree-calf, or padded calf, $3.50.

———— The Lady of the Lake. Students' Edition.
Edited, with Notes and Introduction, by W. J. ROLFE. 1 vol. 12mo.
Beautifully illustrated. 75 cents.

SENSIER'S (ALFRED) Jean-François Millet: Peasant and
Painter. Translated by HELENA DE KAY. With Illustrations. $3.00.

SHALER'S (PROFESSOR N. S.) and *DAVIS'S* (WILLIAM M.)
Illustrations of the Earth's Surface. Part I. Glaciers. Copiously illustrated. Large folio. $10.00.

SHEDD'S (MRS. JULIA A.) Famous Painters and Paintings. Revised edition. With 13 Heliotypes. 1 vol. 12mo. $3.00. Half-
calf, $5.00. Tree-calf, $7.00.

———— Famous Sculptors and Sculpture. With thirteen
Heliotype Engravings. 12mo. $3.00. Half-calf, $5.00. Tree-calf, $7.00.

———— Raphael: His Madonnas and Holy Families.
Illustrated with 22 full-page Heliotypes. 1 vol. 4to. Full gilt. $7.50.

SHERIDAN'S (RICHARD BRINSLEY) Comedies: The
Rivals, and the School for Scandal. Edited, with Biography and Notes and
Introduction, by BRANDER MATTHEWS. Illustrated. 1 vol. 8vo. $3.00.

SHERRATT'S (R. J.) The Elements of Hand-Railing.
38 Plates. Small folio. $2.00.

SIKES'S (WIRT) British Goblins. Welsh Folk-Lore, Fairy
Mythology, and Traditions. Illustrated. 8vo. Gilt top. $4.00.

SNIDER'S (DENTON J.) Agamemnon's Daughter. A
Poem. 1 vol. Square 16mo. Fine laid paper. $1.50.

———————— A Walk in Hellas. 1 vol. 8vo. $2.50.

———————— An Epigrammatic Voyage. A Poem. 1 vol.
Square 16mo. $1.00.

———————— Goethe's Faust: A Commentary. 2 vols.
12mo. $3.50.

SPOONER'S (SAMUEL) and *CLEMENT'S* (MRS. CLARA E.)
A Biographical History of the Fine Arts. *In preparation.*

STANWOOD'S (EDWARD) A History of Presidential Elec-
tions. 1 vol. 12mo. $1.50.

STERNBERG'S (GEORGE M., M.D.) Photo-Micrographs,
and How to Make them. Illustrated by 47 Photographs of Microscopic
Objects, reproduced by the Heliotype process. 1 vol. 8vo. $3.00.

STEVENSON'S (ALEXANDER F.) The Battle of Stone
River, near Murfreesboro', Tenn., December 30, 1862, to January 3, 1863.
1 vol. 8vo. With Maps. $3.00.

STILLMAN'S (DR. J. D. B.) The Horse in Motion, as
Shown in a Series of Views by Instantaneous Photography, and Anatomical
Illustrations in Chromo, after Drawings by WILLIAM HAHN. With a Preface
by LELAND STANFORD. 1 vol. Royal quarto. Fully illustrated. $10.00.

STIRLING'S (A.) At Daybreak. A Novel. 16mo. $1.25.

STOCKTON'S (LOUISE) Dorothea. 1 vol. 16mo. $1.00.
In paper covers, 50 cents.

STODDARD'S (JOHN L.) Red-Letter Days Abroad. 8vo.
With 130 fine Illustrations. Richly bound, full gilt edges, in box. $5.00.
In tree-calf or antique morocco. $10.00. In mosaic inlaid, calf, $12.50.

STONE'S (CHARLES J., F.R.S.L., F.R.Hist.C.) Christianity
before Christ; or, Prototypes of our Faith and Culture. Crown 8vo. $3.00.

STRIKE IN THE B——— MILL (The). A Novel. 16mo.
$1.00. In paper covers, 50 cents.

SWEETSER'S (M. F.) Artist-Biographies. With twelve
Heliotypes in each volume. 5 vols. 16mo. Cloth. Each, $1.50.
    Vol. I. Raphael, Leonardo, Angelo.
    Vol. II. Titian, Guido, Claude.
    Vol. III. Reynolds, Turner, Landseer.
    Vol. IV. Dürer, Rembrandt, Van Dyck.
    Vol. V. Angelico, Murillo, Allston.
The set, in box, 5 vols. $7.50. Half-calf, $15.00. Tree-calf, $25.00.
Flexible calf, elegant leather case, $28.00.

SYLVESTER'S (HERBERT M.) **Prose Pastorals.** 1 vol.
12mo. Gilt top. $1.50.

TENNYSON'S (Lord) A Dream of Fair Women. Forty
Illustrations. 4to. $5.00. In morocco antique or tree-calf, $9.00.

———————— The Princess. Holiday Edition. 120 Illustrations. Rich binding. In a box. 8vo. $6.00. Morocco antique,
flexible calf, or tree-calf, $10.00. Crushed levant, with silk linings, $25.00.

———————— The Princess. Tremont Edition. 1 vol.
16mo. Beautifully illustrated. With red lines, bevelled boards, and gilt
edges, $2.50. Half-calf, $4.00. Antique morocco, flexible calf, flexible seal,
or tree-calf, $5.00.

———————— The Princess. Pocket Edition. 1 vol.
Little-Classic size. With 30 Illustrations. Elegantly bound, $1.00. Half-
calf, $2.25. Antique morocco, flexible calf, or seal, $3.00. Tree-calf, or
padded calf, $3.50.

———————— The Princess. Students' Edition. Edited
with Notes and Introduction, by W. J. Rolfe. 12mo. Illustrated. 75
cents.

———————— **Enoch Arden and Other Poems.** Tre-
mont Edition. 1 vol. 16mo. Beautifully illustrated. With red lines,
bevelled boards and gilt edges, $2.50. Half-calf, $4.00. Tree-calf, antique
morocco, flexible calf, or seal, $5.00.

———————— **Enoch Arden and Other Poems.** Pocket
Edition. 1 vol. Little-Classic size. With thirty illustrations. Elegantly
bound, $1.00. Half-calf, $2.25. Antique morocco, flexible calf, or seal,
$3 00. Tree-calf, or padded calf, $3.50.

———————— **Enoch Arden and Other Poems.** Stu-
dents' Edition. Edited, with Notes and Introduction, by W. J. Rolfe.
Illustrated. 1 vol. 12mo. 75 cents.

TENNYSON, Select Poems of. Students' Edition. Edited,
with Notes and Introduction, by W. J. Rolfe. Beautifully illustrated.
1 vol. 12mo. 75 cents.

———————— **Young People's.** Edited, with Notes and
Introduction, by W. J. Rolfe. Beautifully Illustrated. 1 vol. 12mo.
75 cents.

THACKERAY (William M.), The Ballads of. Complete
illustrated edition. Small quarto. Handsomely bound. $1.50.

THOMAS À KEMPIS'S The Imitation of Christ. 16mo.
Red edges. 300 cuts. $1.50. Flexible calf or morocco, $4.00.
  Pocket edition. Round corners. $1.00. Flexible calf, $3.00.
  Edition de luxe. 8vo. Many full-page etchings, red ruling, etc. Full
leather binding, $9.00. In parchment covers, $5.00.

THOMPSON'S (Maurice) Songs of Fair Weather. $1.50.

———————— A Tallahassee Girl. A Novel. 1 vol. 16mo.
$1.00. In paper covers, 50 cents.

———————— His Second Campaign. A Novel. 1 vol.
16mo. $1.00. In paper covers, 50 cents.

TICKNOR'S AMERICAN GUIDE-BOOKS : Newly re-vised and Augmented Editions.

New England. With nineteen Maps and Plans. Tenth edition. 16mo. $1.50.

The Maritime Provinces. With ten Maps and Plans. Sixth edition. 16mo. $1.50.

The White Mountains. With six Maps and six Panoramas. Seventh edition. 16mo. $1.50.

The Middle States. With twenty-two Maps and Plans. 16mo. *Seventh Edition in preparation.*

TICKNOR'S PAPER SERIES of Choice Copyright Reading. A series of handsome and attractive books for leisure-hour and railroad reading, made up of some of the choicest and most successful novels of late years, with several entirely new novels by well-known and popular writers. The following are the titles of the first numbers : —

1. **The Story of Margaret Kent.** By HENRY HAYES.
2. **Guenn.** By BLANCHE W. HOWARD, Author of " One Summer."
3. **The Cruise of a Woman Hater.** By G. DE MONTAUBAN.
4. **A Reverend Idol.** A Massachusetts Coast Romance.
5. **A Nameless Nobleman.** By JANE G. AUSTIN.
6. **The Prelate.** A Roman Story. By ISAAC HENDERSON.
7. **Eleanor Maitland.** By CLARA ERSKINE CLEMENT.
8. **The House of the Musician.** By VIRGINIA W. JOHNSON, author of " Neptune's Vase," etc.
9. **Geraldine.** A metrical romance of the St. Lawrence.
10. **The Duchess Emilia.** By BARRETT WENDELL.
11. **Dr. Breen's Practice.** By W. D. HOWELLS.
12. **Tales of Three Cities.** By HENRY JAMES.
13. **The House at High Bridge.** By EDGAR FAWCETT.
14. **The Story of a Country Town.** By E. W. HOWE.
15. **The Confessions of a Frivolous Girl.** By ROBERT GRANT.
16. **Culture's Garland.** By EUGENE FIELD.
17. **Patty's Perversities.** By ARLO BATES.
18. **A Modern Instance.** By WM. D. HOWELLS.

Issued semi-monthly. Price per number, fifty cents. Subscription price, postage-paid, $12.00 per annum, 24 numbers.

TIERNAN'S (MRS. MARY F.) Homoselle. A Novel. 1 vol. 16mo. $1.00. In paper covers, 50 cents.

TOWLE'S (GEORGE MAKEPEACE) England and Russia in Central Asia. No. 1, Timely-Topics Series. 1 vol. 16mo. With Maps. 50 cents.

————— England in Egypt. No. 2, Timely-Topics Series. 1 vol. 16mo. With Maps. 50 cents.

TOWNSEND'S (MARY ASHLEY) Down the Bayou. A volume of Poems. 12mo. $1.50.

————————— (S. NUGENT) Our Indian Summer in the Far West. With full-page Photographs of Scenes in Kansas, Colorado, New Mexico, Texas, etc. 4to. $20.00.

TWO GENTLEMEN OF BOSTON. A Novel. 12mo. $1.50.

UNDERWOOD'S (FRANCIS H.) John Greenleaf Whittier.
A Biography. 1 vol. 12mo. Illustrated. $1.50.

———————————— Henry Wadsworth Longfellow. 12mo.
Illustrated. $1.50.

———————————— James Russell Lowell. A Biographical
Sketch. 1 vol. Small quarto. 6 Heliotypes. $1.50.

VENTURA'S (L. D.) and *S. SHEVITCH'S* **Misfits and**
Remnants. A volume of short stories. 1 vol. 16mo. $1.00.

VIOLLET-LE-DUC'S (E. E.) Discourses on Architecture.
With many Steel Plates and Chromos, and hundreds of Woodcuts. 2 vols.
8vo. $15.00.

VIRGINIA CAMPAIGN (THE) OF GEN. POPE IN
1862. Being Vol. II. of Papers read before the Military Historical Society
of Massachusetts. With Maps and Plans. 1 vol. 8vo. $3.00.

WALLACE'S (MRS. LEW.) The Storied Sea. 1 vol. Little-
Classic size. $1.00.

WARE'S (PROFESSOR WILLIAM R.) Modern Perspective.
A Treatise upon the Principles and Practice of Plane and Cylindrical Perspective. 1 vol. 12mo. With Portfolio of 27 Plates. $5.00.

WARING'S (COL. GEORGE E., JR.) Whip and Spur.
Little-Classic size. $1.25. Large Paper Edition, $4.00.

———————————— Village Improvements and Farm Villages.
Little-Classic size. Illustrated. 75 cents.

———————————— The Bride of the Rhine. Two Hundred Miles
in a Mosel Row-Boat. To which is added a paper on the Latin poet
Ausonius and his poem "Mosella," by Rev. CHARLES T. BROOKS. 1 vol.
Square 16mo. Fully illustrated. $1.50. Large Paper Edition, $4.00.

———————————— Vix. No. 1 of Waring's Horse-Stories. 10 cents.

———————————— Ruby. No. 2 of Waring's Horse-Stories. 10 cents.

WARNER'S (CHARLES DUDLEY) The American Newspaper. 32mo. 25 cents.

WARREN'S (JOSEPH H., M.D.) A Plea for the Cure of
Rupture. 12mo. In cloth, $1.25. In parchment paper covers, $1.00.

———————————— A Practical Treatise on Hernia. 8vo. $5.00.
In sheep, $6.50.

WEDGWOOD'S (HENSLEIGH) Contested Etymologies in
the Dictionary of the Rev. W. W. SKEAT. 1 vol. 12mo. $2.00.

WEEKS'S (LYMAN H.) Among the Azores. 1 vol. Square
16mo. With Map and 25 Illustrations. $1.50.

WELLS'S (KATE GANNETT) About People. A volume of
Essays. Little-Classic size. $1.25.

WENDELL'S (BARRETT) **Rankell's Remains.** An American Novel. $1.00.

———————————— The Duchess Emilia. $1.00. In Ticknor's
Paper Series, 50 cents.

WERTHEIMBER'S (Louis) **A Muramasa Blade.** A
Story of Feudalism in Old Japan. Beautifully illustrated by Japanese
artists. 8vo. Gilt top and rough edges. $3.00. Bound in red Kioto silk
brocade, $5.00.

WHEELER'S (Charles Gardner) The Course of Em-
pire; Being Outlines of the Chief Political Changes in the History of the
World. 1 vol. 8vo. With 25 colored Maps. $3.00. Half-calf, $5.50.
New and cheaper edition. 12mo. $2.00.

———— (William A. and Charles G.) Familiar
Allusions: A Handbook of Miscellaneous Information. 12mo. $3.00.
Half-calf, $5.50.
New and cheaper edition. 12mo. $2.00.

WHIPPLE'S (Edwin Percy) **American Literature and
Other Papers.** With an Introduction by John Greenleaf Whittier,
to whom the volume is dedicated. 1 vol. 12mo. Gilt top. $1.50. Half-
calf, $3.00.

———— **Recollections of Eminent Men.** (Sumner,
Motley, Agassiz, Choate, etc.) With Portrait, and Dr. Bartol's Memorial
Address. $1.50; in half-calf, $3.00.

WHIST, American or Standard. By G. W. P. Seventh
edition. Revised and enlarged. 16mo. $1.00.

WHIST, Universal. An Analysis of the Game, improved
by the Introduction of American Leads. By G. W. P., author of "American Whist." 1 vol. Gilt top. $1.25.

WHITING'S (Charles Goodrich) **The Saunterer.**
Essays on Nature. Illustrated. 16mo. $1.25.

WILLIAMS'S (Alfred M.) The Poets and Poetry of Ire-
land. With Critical Essays and Notes. 1 vol. 12mo. $2.00.

WINCKELMANN'S (John) The History of Ancient Art.
Translated by Dr. G. H. Lodge. With 78 copperplate Engravings. 2 vols.
8vo. $9.00. Half-calf, $18.00. Morocco antique or tree-calf, $25.00.

WINTER'S (William) English Rambles, and other Fugi-
tive Pieces in Prose and Verse. 1 vol. 12mo. $1.50.

———— Poems. New revised edition. 1 vol. 16mo.
Cloth, $1.50. Half-calf, $3.00. Morocco antique or tree-calf, $4.00.

———— The Trip to England. With Illustrations by
Joseph Jefferson. 16mo. $2.00. Half-calf, $4.00. Morocco antique or
tree-calf, $5.00.

———— Shakespeare's England. 1 vol. 24mo. 50 cents.

WITHERSPOON'S (Rev. Orlando) Doctor Ben. A
Novel. 1 vol. 16mo. $1.00. In paper covers, 50 cents.

WOODS'S (Rev. Leonard) History of the Andover Theo-
logical Seminary. 1 vol. 8vo. $3.50.

TICKNOR'S PAPER SERIES

OF

CHOICE COPYRIGHT NOVELS.

A series of handsome and attractive books for leisure-hour reading, made up of some of the choicest and most successful novels of late years, with several entirely new novels by well-known and popular writers.

No. 1. **The Story of Margaret Kent.** By HENRY HAYES.

No. 2. **Guenn.** By BLANCHE W. HOWARD, author of "One Summer."

No. 3. **The Cruise of a Woman-Hater.** By G. DE MONTAUBAN.

No. 4. **A Reverend Idol.** A Romance of the Massachusetts Coast.

No. 5. **A Nameless Nobleman.** By JANE G. AUSTIN.

No. 6. **The Prelate.** By ISAAC HENDERSON. A Roman Story.

No. 7. **Eleanor Maitland.** By CLARA ERSKINE CLEMENT.

No 8. **The House of the Musician.** By VIRGINIA W. JOHNSON.

No. 9. **Geraldine.** A metrical romance of the St. Lawrence.

No. 10. **The Duchess Emilia.** By BARRETT WENDELL.

No. 11. **Dr. Breen's Practice.** By W. D. HOWELLS.

No. 12. **Tales of Three Cities.** By HENRY JAMES.

No. 13. **The House at High Bridge.** By EDGAR FAWCETT.

No. 14. **The Story of a Country Town.** By E. W. HOWE.

No. 15. **The Confessions of a Frivolous Girl.** By ROBERT GRANT, author of "Face to Face," "A Romantic Young Lady," etc.

No. 16. **Culture's Garland:** Being Memoranda of the Gradual Rise of Literature, Art, Music, and Society in Chicago and other Western Ganglia. By EUGENE FIELD.

No. 17. **Patty's Perversities.** By ARLO BATES, author of "The Pagans," "A Wheel of Fire," etc.

No. 18. **A Modern Instance.** By W. D. HOWELLS, author of "The Rise of Silas Lapham," etc. The career of Bartley Hubbard, a Boston journalist, and a study of conjugal life in modern America.

Price per number, 50 cents. Annual Subscriptions for 24 Numbers, $12.00. Issued Semi-monthly.

Entered at the Post-Office Boston, as Second-Class Matter.

NEW BOOKS

TO BE PUBLISHED DURING THE AUTUMN OF

1887.

The Prices named below are subject to Revision on Publication.

Uniform with " Lucile," " The Lady of the Lake," &c.

SCOTT'S THE LAY OF THE LAST MINSTREL. } Tremont
TENNYSON'S ENOCH ARDEN, Etc. } edition.
Each in 1 vol. 16mo. Beautifully illustrated. With red lines, bevelled boards, and gilt edges, $2.50; half-calf, $4.00; tree-calf, antique morocco, or flexible calf or seal, $5.00.

SCOTT'S THE LAY OF THE LAST MINSTREL. } Pocket
TENNYSON'S ENOCH ARDEN, Etc. } edition.
Each in 1 vol. Little-Classic size. With thirty illustrations. Elegantly bound, $1.00; half-calf, $2.25; antique morocco, or flexible calf or seal, $3.00; tree-calf, padded calf, $3.50.

These new and beautiful editions of these perennially popular poems are made from *entirely new electrotype-plates*, in large and easily legible type, with more than thirty exquisite illustrations. As these are the newest, handsomest, and cheapest, they cannot fail to become the best-selling editions in the market.

THE LONGFELLOW PROSE BIRTHDAY BOOK; OR, LONG-FELLOW'S DAYS. Being extracts from his journals and letters, edited by MRS. LAURA WINTHROP JOHNSON. 1 vol. Beautifully illustrated and bound. 1 vol. 18mo. Cloth, $1.00; flexible calf or seal, $2.50.

Mrs. Johnson has capitally worked out the charming notion of selecting from Longfellow's letters and journals, sentiments and appropriate thoughts, many of them written for the very day, and constructing for the year a new birthday book, prose only in form, so full it is of the spirit of poetry.

AN OPERETTA IN PROFILE. By CZEIKA. 1 vol. 16mo. $1.00.
Some years since, the author was one of the most popular magazine writers; but long residence abroad and other circumstances compelled him, for a time, to abandon writing. He now comes forward with this remarkable production, which is sure to command wide attention. It is forcible, terse, satirical. It deals with social follies, is bright and fascinating. It will at once impress the reader as the work of a writer of great intellectual power.

THREE GOOD GIANTS. From the French of François Rabelais. By JOHN DIMITRY 1 vol. Square 12mo. With 175 illustrations by Gustave Doré and A. Robida. $1.50.

The peculiarities that have hitherto rendered Rabelais a sealed book for the young have been wholly eliminated in this work, but with so much skill as not to impair the continuity of the story. It will take its place at once beside the Arabian Nights and Gulliver's Travels — which both require similar editing — and will serve a good purpose in disarming much unreasoning prejudice against Rabelais, while opening to the delighted eyes of the young the true stories of Grandgousier, Gargantua, and Pantagruel, the quaintest and most original of giants, and of Panurge, the funniest of jokers. The illustrations by Doré and Robida are a delight and wonder in themselves.

BEAUTIFUL HOLIDAY BOOKS.

GERALDINE. A tale of the St. Lawrence. 1 vol. 8vo. Beautifully illustrated, full gilt, $3 50; in antique morocco, tree or flexible calf, $7.50.

The extraordinary popularity of Geraldine, the extreme interest and delicacy of the love story it enshrines, and the vivid and accurate pictures of scenery of the Great Lakes, the Thousand Islands, the St. Lawrence and Saguenay Rivers, etc., have indicated the book as especially appropriate for illustration. The scenes depicted in the poem have been drawn from nature by a special artist, who visited them for that purpose, and followed the routes of Trent and his friends. The other illustrations are by the best American artists, and the whole in beautiful and appropriate binding forms one of the best and most popular and attractive gifts or keepsakes for the holiday season, or for any other.

THE POETICAL WORKS OF SIR WALTER SCOTT. Revised, corrected, and edited, with notes and commentaries, by WILLIAM J. ROLFE, editor of the "Students' Series of Classic Poems," "Students' Shakespeare," etc. 1 vol. 8vo. With 350 illustrations. Bevelled boards. Full gilt, $10 00; half calf, $13.00; tree-calf, or antique morocco, $10.00.

ALL EXISTING EDITIONS of Sir Walter Scott's poetry or single poems, except those issued by Ticknor & Co., are disfigured and rendered untrustworthy throughout by gross and numerous errors and misprints. Mr. W. J. Rolfe, the accomplished editor of the "Students' Series of Poetry " and of Shakespeare, has undertaken the herculean task of editing and restoring the correct and original text, and of producing in one volume **the first and only correct edition** in England or America of Scott's Poems. The edition will contain full notes and appendices with preface and comments by Mr. Rolfe. It also contains all the original illustrations made for the separate poems at a cost of upwards of **twenty-five thousand dollars**, besides many others especially added for this work, nearly three hundred and fifty in all. The popularity of Scott's poetry, the unique position of this edition for scholarship and accuracy, and the number, variety, and excellence of the illustrations combine to assure for this book immediate popularity and a permanent standing.

Two Beautiful and Popular Books.

MY OLD KENTUCKY HOME.   THE SWANEE RIVER. By STEPHEN COLLINS FOSTER. Beautifully illustrated. Each in one volume. 4to. Full gilt. Cloth, ivory finish, imitation wood or monkey grain, $1.50; seal, $2.50; flexible calf, extra, or tree-calf, $5.00.

No one like Stephen Foster has ever had the power to reach and touch every heart. He united to simple words, usually in dialect, music of a peculiar pathos and tenderness that appealed to all men, which has won for him a unique and special place not granted to the work of other composers. Millions of these, his best songs, have been circulated; but never before has the artist's pencil been enlisted to adorn the ballads that have pleased and softened so many hearts. The drawings have been made and engraved by the best artists with the utmost care, and will be found apt and worthy illustrations of these tender and beautiful songs.

THE STORY OF AN ENTHUSIAST. Told by Himself. A Novel, by MRS. C. V. JAMISON, author of "Woven of Many Threads," "A Crown from the Spear," etc. 1 vol. 12mo, $1.50.

A new novel by the distinguished author of "Woven of Many Threads" (known through her former books as MRS. HAMILTON) is sure to be warmly welcomed. "The Story of an Enthusiast" is a finely written and harmonious work, and is replete with interest.

THE NEW ASTRONOMY. By S. P. LANGLEY. 1 vol. 8vo. Illustrated, $5 00.

A most fascinating as well as instructive volume, giving the latest discoveries and theories in Astronomical Science, with many elaborate and beautiful illustrations.

THE PILGRIM REPUBLIC. A Historical Review of the Colony of New Plymouth, with sketches of the rise of other New England settlements, the History of Congregationalism, and the creeds of the period. By JOHN A. GOODWIN. 1 vol. 8vo. Maps and plans, $4.00.

A careful and thorough history of the founding and growth of the Plymouth Colony, the result of many years' labor by the late author, which will be found indispensable to all libraries, public and private, and to all readers who desire to study the history of their own country.

A MAN STORY. A new novel by E W. HOWE, author of "The Story of a Country Town," "A Moonlight Boy," etc., $1.50.

A HISTORY OF THE SECESSION WAR. By ROSSITER JOHNSON. 1 vol. With Maps and Diagrams.

A compact and careful account of the war and the causes that led to it. The principal portion of this work was published serially and received with the greatest approval. It has now been revised and enlarged, and forms a complete and compact as well as accurate and entertaining history of the Rebellion.

MUSIC IN THE EIGHTEENTH CENTURY. Collected and edited by HENRY M. BROOKS, editor of the "Olden-Time Series," with an introduction by EDWARD S. MORSE. 1 vol. 12mo. Illustrated $1.00.

The editor of the popular "Olden-Time Series" has here collected in a larger volume many rare and curious anecdotes, ana, etc., about music and musicians, of interest to all, and especially to music lovers.

LOVE AND THEOLOGY. A Novel, by CELIA PARKER WOOLLEY. 1 vol. 12mo, $1.50.

A novel and brilliant story by a new and talented writer. It is not only entertaining as a story, but engrosses interest from the highest ethical standpoint. . . . It is most decidedly a book to *own*, and not merely to read for amusement only and then throw aside."

THE BHAGAVAD-GÌTÀ; OR, THE LORD'S LAY. With Commentary and notes, as well as references to the Christian Scriptures, Translated from the Sanskrit for the benefit of those in search of spiritual light, by MOHINI M. CHATTERJI, M. A. 1 vol. 8vo. Gilt top, $2.00

NEW AND CHEAPER EDITIONS

OF

POPULAR, STANDARD, AND ILLUSTRATED BOOKS.

POETS AND ETCHERS. A volume of full-page etchings, by JAMES D. SMILLIE, SAMUEL COLMAN, A. F. BELLOWS, H. FARRER, and R. SWAIN GIFFORD, illustrating poems by Longfellow, Whittier, Bryant, Aldrich, etc. 4to. A new edition in new binding. Full gilt, $5.00.

THE TICKNOR SERIES OF OCTAVO POETS.

LIBRARY EDITION.

"LUCILE," by OWEN MEREDITH.

"THE LADY OF THE LAKE," by SIR WALTER SCOTT.

"THE LAY OF THE LAST MINSTREL," by SIR WALTER SCOTT.

"MARMION," by SIR WALTER SCOTT.

"THE PRINCESS," by ALFRED LORD TENNYSON.

"CHILDE HAROLD," by LORD BYRON.

Six volumes, elegantly and uniformly bound, with all the original illustrations, bevelled boards and full gilt in cloth. Each, $3.50; in tree-calf or flexible calf, extra, $7.50.

These are the most famous and popular editions in existence of these great poems. In their original shape, they have had enormous sales, and in their cheaper form, with all their original illustrations, complete and unworn, they will have renewed popularity.

Also uniform with the above, in style and price, the beautifully illustrated

TUSCAN CITIES. By W. D. HOWELLS.

RED-LETTER DAYS ABROAD. By JOHN L. STODDARD.

SONNETS FROM THE PORTUGUESE. By ELIZABETH BARRETT BROWNING. Illustrated by Ludvig Sandoë Ipsen. 1 vol. Oblong quarto, beautifully bound, full gilt, $8.00.

This magnificent work was a labor of love for years with the artist, who has made a series of designs, the equals of which as a mere treasury of decoration and invention, apart from their significance in illustrating the immortal verse of Mrs. Browning, have never been issued in America.

THE CORRESPONDENCE OF THOMAS CARLYLE AND RALPH WALDO EMERSON.

NATHANIEL HAWTHORNE AND HIS WIFE.

New and cheaper editions, each in two volumes. 12mo. With portraits and other illustrations. Per set, $3.00.

JAPANESE HOMES. By PROF. EDWARD S. MORSE.

CHOSON: THE LAND OF THE MORNING CALM. B PERCIVAL LOWELL.

Each in 1 vol. Large 8vo. Illustrated. Per vol., $3.00.

FOOLS OF NATURE. A Novel. 1 vol. 12mo, $1.50.

A strong and original work. It is anti-spiritualistic in fact, while yet showing how some trusting natures honestly follow such beliefs. There are many finely drawn scenes and figures in the book, a great deal of careful analysis of character and motive, much both of pathos and passion, the whole life-like and well drawn.

A SEA CHANGE; OR, LOVE'S STOWAWAY. A comic opera. By WILLIAM D. HOWELLS. 1 vol. 16mo. Little-Classic size, $1.00.

SOBRIQUETS AND NICKNAMES. By ALBERT R. FREY. 1 vol. Crown 8vo, half morocco, gilt top, library style, $3.50.

Some years ago, the author, while engaged upon a dictionary of Pseudo-nyms (since incorporated in Mr. Cushing's work), found so many nicknames, etc., that he began to collect them. The result is the present volume, containing over *five thousand subjects*, and is invaluable to all libraries, editors, students, and to all who find such books as Wheeler's, Brewer's, or Cushing's useful in their reading, study, or work.

A FLOCK OF GIRLS. A book for girls. By NORA PERRY, author of "After the Ball," etc. 1 vol. 12mo, $1.50.

Miss Perry is one of the most popular writers for girls, and her stories for them are eagerly sought by all the best editors. This volume contains her best and latest stories, and is sure of a warm reception.

JUAN AND JUANITA. By FRANCES COURTENAY BAYLOR, author of "On Both Sides," etc. 1 vol. Square 4to. With many illustrations, by HENRY SANDHAM, $1.50.

Miss Baylor's charming and "ower true" tale has formed the chief attraction of the "St. Nicholas" for a year, and in complete form, and with considerable additions, will be heartily welcomed, most of all by those who have already learned to love its little hero and heroine, and eagerly look for the full story of their adventures.

UNDER PINE AND PALM. Poems by MRS. FRANCES L. MACE, author of "Legends, Lyrics and Sonnets," "Israfil," "Only Waiting," etc. 1 vol. 12mo, $1.75.

"Only Waiting" was written by Mrs. Mace at the age of about sixteen, and attracted wide attention. Her more recent poems have been published in the leading magazines, and are acknowledged to be among the finest gems of American poetry. The beauty of her verse is unquestioned, and it is safe to predict that "Under Pine and Palm" will be widely read.

NEW WAGGINGS OF OLD TALES. By Two Wags. 1 vol. Illustrated.

A volume of burlesque novelettes, etc., by a combination of wits, sure to be found amusing and popular.

AGATHA PAGE. A new novel by ISAAC HENDERSON, author of "The Prelate." 1 vol. 12mo, $1.50.

A new story by the author of "The Prelate" is sure to be promptly and permanently popular.

A NEW VOLUME OF ESSAYS. From the papers of EDWIN PERCY WHIPPLE, author of "Recollections of Eminent Men," "American Literature," etc. 1 vol. 12mo. Gilt top, $1.50.

STEADFAST. A Novel, by ROSE TERRY COOKE, author of "Somebody's Neighbors," etc. 12mo, $1.50.

STORIES AND SKETCHES. By JOHN BOYLE O'REILLY, editor of the *Pilot*, author of "Moondyne," "Songs, Legends, Ballads," etc. 1 vol. 12mo, $1.50.

The great popularity of the author, and the intrinsic merit and interest of his writings, will insure a warm reception to this collection of his latest and best works.

A NOVEL. By EDWARD BELLAMY, author of "Miss Ludington's Sister." 1 vol. 12mo, $1.50.

A NOVEL. By MISS L. G. NOBLE, author of "A Reverend Idol." 1 vol. 12mo, $1.50.

SAFE BUILDING. By LOUIS DE COPPET BERG. 1 vol. Square 8vo, $5.00.

These papers are the work of a practising *architect*, and not that of a mere book-maker or theorist. Mr. Berg, aiming to make his work of the greatest value to the largest number, has confined himself in his mathematical demonstrations to the use of arithmetic, algebra, and plane geometry. In short, these papers are in the highest sense *practical and valuable*.

A NEW AND ENLARGED CONCORDANCE TO THE HOLY SCRIPTURES. By REV. J. B. R. WALKER.

This monumental work of patient industry and iron diligence is indispensable to all students of the Bible, to which it is the key and introduction. Many errors and omissions in the plans of the older Concordances have been avoided in this one: which also bears reference to the Revised Bible, as well as to the King James version.

THE OLDEN-TIME SERIES. Edited by HENRY M. BROOKS, with many illustrations and fac-similes. Six volumes in two, $2.50.

A new, compact edition of these popular collections of anecdote and incident.

THE LATEST PUBLICATIONS.

CULTURE'S GARLAND: Being Memoranda of the Gradual Rise of Literature, Art, Music, and Society in Chicago and other Western Ganglia. By EUGENE FIELD. Paper, 50 cents; cloth, $1.00.

PENELOPE'S SUITORS. By EDWIN LASSETTER BYNNER. 1 vol. 32mo. Quaintly bound in antique paper boards, with strings. 50 cts.

This captivating story of the old Colony days in Massachusetts was originally published serially, when it aroused wide attention and great admiration. In deference to a public demand, it is now brought out in a quaint and dainty little volume, making one of the prettiest and most *bijou*-like books of the year. The Boston "Daily Advertiser" pronounces it: "A subtly-clever, original, and remarkably well-told story. The way in which the Governor steals the heart of 'the young gentlewoman,' just at a time when she is about to become engaged to a young friend of his, is sketched with exquisite grace and charm."

PROSE PASTORALS. By HERBERT M. SYLVESTER. 1 vol. 12mo. Gilt top. $1.50.

A series of very charming chapters on Nature and the manifold attractions of rural life, and rambling in the forests and meadows. No better companion can be found for a summer day in the country. It is an entirely new work, the result and crystallization of years of communion with Nature.

HOME SANITATION. A Manual for Housekeepers. By the Sanitary Science Club of the Association of Collegiate Alumnæ. Cloth. 50 cents.

The object of this manual is to arouse the interest of housekeepers in the sanitary conditions of their homes, and to indicate the points requiring investigation, the methods of examination, and the practical remedies. The subjects treated are the situation of the house, care of the cellar, plumbing and drainage, ventilation, heating, lighting, furnishing, clothing, food and drink. Each topic is introduced by an explanatory statement, which is followed by a series of questions so framed that an affirmative answer implies a satisfactory arrangement; and they also suggest a remedy if the answer is negative.

FINAL MEMORIALS OF HENRY WADSWORTH LONG-FELLOW. By SAMUEL LONGFELLOW, author of "Life of Henry Wadsworth Longfellow," etc. 1 vol. 8vo. Uniform with the "Life." With two new steel plates, and other illustrations. Cloth, $3.00; half calf, with marbled edges, $5.50; half morocco, with gilt top and rough edges, $5.50.

The volume contains the journals and letters of the last twelve years of the poet's life, which were omitted from the Biography through fear of making it unduly large, their places being there supplied by a summary narrative. Many letters are also given of the earlier periods, from Mr Longfellow and his correspondents, such as Mr. T G. Appleton, Mr. J. L. Motley, Dean Stanley, etc. There is a chapter of "table talk" and some pieces of unpublished verse; the tributes of Prof. C. C. Everett, Dr. O. W. Holmes, and Prof. C. E. Norton are given, and extracts from the reminiscences of Mr. William Winter and others An Appendix contains genealogical and bibliographical matter. The work contains impressions of two engraved portraits and a vignette, prepared expressly for this edition. There are also full-page wood-engravings of several "Longfellow" houses, and curious fac-similes of drawings and sketches, and pencil portraits of Mr. Longfellow hitherto unknown.

THE DEVIL'S HAT. By MELVILLE PHILIPS. 1 vol. 12mo. $1.00.

A novel of intense and absorbing interest, whose scenes are laid in the oil regions of Pennsylvania, — a sufficiently novel and attractive field for romance. As a vigorous critic has written, "Much of the real worth of the book lies in the accurate picture of life in the oil regions. This part of the work is *very* finely done. The various incidents of such a life are all realistically written, while the scenery of the tale is sketched with an artistic hand."

LIGHTS AND SHADOWS OF A LIFE. By MADELEINE VINTON DAHLGREN (Mrs. Admiral Dahlgren), author of "A Washington Winter," "South-Sea Sketches," "South-Mountain Magic," "Memoirs of Admiral Dahlgren," etc. 1 vol. 12mo. $1.50.

The novel, a Southern tale, is written in the same powerful and fascinating manner that has won for Mrs. Dahlgren's published works such remarkable popularity and success, and is pronounced the best work yet written by this distinguished lady. The picture of Southern home life, the unveiling of the secrets of a heart, the coming and going of the lights and shadows in the heroine's life, are portrayed in Mrs. Dahlgren's most perfect manner, and form but small parts of one of the most successful and delightful novels of the season.

THE SUNNY SIDE OF SHADOW—Reveries of a Convalescent. By Mrs. S. G. W. BENJAMIN. 1 vol. 16mo. $1.00.

LETTERS OF HORATIO GREENOUGH to his Brother, Henry Greenough. With Biographical Sketches, and some Contemporary Correspondence. Edited by FRANCES BOOTT GREENOUGH. 1 vol. 12mo. With Portrait. $1.25.

"Very welcome to readers of literary tastes and artistic sympathies. They give one a portrait of a sensitive nature, keenly alive to whatever was fine and true. The letters throw side-lights on the growth of art and artistic tastes in America, and have a distinct value on that account. There are letters from Willis, Dana, the Greenoughs, *et als.*, with charming pictures of Boston fifty years ago."

NIGHTS WITH UNCLE REMUS: Myths and Legends of the Old Plantation. By JOEL CHANDLER HARRIS, Author of "Uncle Remus: his Songs and Sayings," "At Teague Poteet's," etc. 1 vol. 16mo. Illustrated. Paper covers. 50 cents.

This is the choicest of Harris's inimitable books of Southern life, legends, and dialect, which have met with such extraordinarily large sales. In answer to the great popular demand, this new edition in paper covers has been brought out.

THE NIGRITIANS. Division One of the Social History of the Races of Mankind. By A. FEATHERMAN. 1 vol. 8vo. $6.00.

THE MELANESIANS. Division Two of the Social History of the Races of Mankind. By A. FEATHERMAN. 1 vol. 8vo. $6.00.

REFERENCE BOOKS.

FAMILIAR SHORT SAYINGS OF GREAT MEN. By S. ARTHUR BENT, A.M. Fifth edition. 12mo. Vellum, cloth. $2.00.

Indispensable to students, writers, and libraries. It gives a collection of short, sententious sayings of all times, such as are constantly referred to.

THE COURSE OF EMPIRE. Being Outlines of the Chief Political Changes in the History of the World. Arranged by Centuries, by C. G. WHEELER. With 25 maps. 1 vol. 12mo. $2.00.

FAMILIAR ALLUSIONS. A Handbook of Miscellaneous Information, including the names of Celebrated Statues, Paintings, Palaces, Country Seats, Ruins, Churches, Ships, Streets, Clubs, Natural Curiosities, and the like. By WILLIAM A. WHEELER and CHARLES G. WHEELER. 1 vol. 12mo. $2.00.

EVENTS AND EPOCHS IN RELIGIOUS HISTORY. By JAMES FREEMAN CLARKE, D.D. Illustrated. 12mo. $2.00.

EDGE-TOOLS OF SPEECH. By MATURIN M. BALLOU. $3.50. An encyclopædia of quotations, the brightest sayings of the wise and famous. Invaluable for debating societies, writers, and public speakers. A treasure for libraries.

An almost inexhaustible mine of the choicest thoughts of the best writers of all ages and countries, from Confucius down to Garfield and Gladstone,— a *pot-pourri* of all the spiciest ingredients of literature. There is a vacancy on every student's desk and in every library which it alone can fill, and soon will fill. The book deserves its popularity.— *The Northwestern.*

THE

MEMORIAL HISTORY OF BOSTON,

In Four Volumes. Quarto.

With more than 500 Illustrations by famous artists and engravers, all made for this work.

Edited by JUSTIN WINSOR, LIBRARIAN OF HARVARD UNIVERSITY.

Among the contributors are : —

Gov. JOHN D. LONG,	Dr. O. W. HOLMES,
Hon. CHARLES FRANCIS ADAMS,	JOHN G. WHITTIER,
Rev. PHILLIPS BROOKS, D.D.,	Rev. J. F. CLARKE, D.D.,
Rev. E. E. HALE, D.D.,	Rev. A. P. PEABODY, D.D.,
Hon. ROBERT C. WINTHROP,	Col. T. W. HIGGINSON,
Hon. J. HAMMOND TRUMBULL,	Professor ASA GRAY,
Admiral G. H. PREBLE,	Gen. F. W. PALFREY,

HENRY CABOT LODGE.

VOLUME I. treats of the Geology, Fauna, and Flora; the Voyages and Maps of the Northmen, Italians, Captain John Smith, and the Plymouth Settlers; the Massachusetts Company, Puritanism, and the Aborigines; the Literature, Life, and Chief Families of the Colonial Period.

VOL. II. treats of the Royal Governors; French and Indian Wars; Witches and Pirates; The Religion, Literature, Customs, and Chief Families of the Provincial Period.

VOL. III. treats of the Revolutionary Period and the Conflict around Boston; and the Statesmen, Sailors, and Soldiers, the Topography, Literature, and Life of Boston during that time; and also of the Last Hundred Years' History, the War of 1812, Abolitionism, and the Press.

VOL. IV. treats of the Social Life, Topography, and Landmarks, Industries Commerce, Railroads, and Financial History of this Century in Boston; with Monographic Chapters on Boston's Libraries, Women, Science, Art, Music, Philosophy, Architecture, Charities, etc.

*** *Sold by subscription only. Send for a Prospectus to the Publishers,*

TICKNOR AND COMPANY, Boston.

THE TICKNOR EDITIONS OF STANDARD ENGLISH POEMS.

ILLUSTRATED OCTAVO EDITIONS.

These choicest editions of the great modern poems were drawn and engraved under the care of A. V. S. ANTHONY. Each in one vol., 8vo, elegantly bound, with full gilt edges, in a neat box. Each poem,

In cloth $6.00
In antique morocco, padded calf, or tree-calf 10.00
In crushed levant, extra, with silk linings 25.00

Scott's The Lay of the Last Minstrel.
Tennyson's The Princess.   Meredith's Lucile.
Scott's The Lady of the Lake.   Scott's Marmion.
Byron's Childe Harold.

LIBRARY EDITIONS.

Lucile.   Marmion.
The Lady of the Lake.   Childe Harold.
The Princess.   The Lay of the Last Minstrel.

Each in one volume, 8vo, elegantly and uniformly bound, with all the original illustrations, bevelled boards, full gilt edges. In cloth . . $3.50
In tree-calf, or flexible calf, extra 7.50

TREMONT EDITIONS.

Lucile.   Marmion.
The Lady of the Lake.   Childe Harold.
The Princess.   ·   The Lay of the Last Minstrel.
Enoch Arden, and Other Poems.

Each in one volume, 16mo, beautifully illustrated. With red lines, bevelled boards, and gilt edges. In cloth $2.50
In half-calf 4.00
In antique morocco, flexible calf, seal or tree-calf 5.00

POCKET EDITIONS.

Lucile.   Marmion.
The Lady of the Lake.   Childe Harold.
The Princess.   The Lay of the Last Minstrel.
Enoch Arden, and Other Poems.

Each in one volume, Little-Classic size. Handsomely and appropriately bound, with many fine illustrations. In cloth $1.00
In half-calf 2.25
In antique morocco, flexible calf, or seal 3.00
In tree-calf, or padded calf 3.50

THE STUDENTS' EDITIONS.

The Lay of the Last Minstrel.   Marmion.
Young People's Tennyson.   The Princess.
Select Poems of Tennyson.   Childe Harold.
Enoch Arden, and Other Poems.   The Lady of the Lake.

Each in one volume. 12mo. Edited, with introduction and copious notes, by W. J. ROLFE. Beautifully illustrated. Red edges. Each volume . . . . $.75

Reprint Publishing

FOR PEOPLE WHO GO FOR ORIGINALS.

This book is a facsimile reprint of the original edition. The term refers to the facsimile with an original in size and design exactly matching simulation as photographic or scanned reproduction.

Facsimile editions offer us the chance to join in the library of historical, cultural and scientific history of mankind, and to rediscover.

The books of the facsimile edition may have marks, notations and other marginalia and pages with errors contained in the original volume. These traces of the past refers to the historical journey that has covered the book.

ISBN 978-3-95940-064-0

Facsimile reprint of the original edition
Copyright © 2015 Reprint Publishing
All rights reserved.

www.reprintpublishing.com

www.ingramcontent.com/pod-product-compliance
Lightning Source LLC
Chambersburg PA
CBHW051647260626
47170CB00004B/1378

* 9 7 8 1 6 3 7 4 7 1 1 8 0 *